A Medieval Bride Novella

THE CLAIMING OF

Lady Joanna

The CLAN MACLERIE Series:
Taming the Highlander
Surrender to the Highlander
Possessed by the Highlander
Taming The Highland Rogue
The Highlander's Stolen Touch
The Forbidden Highlander (novella)
At The Highlander's Mercy
The Highlander's Dangerous Temptation
Yield to The Highlander
The Highlander's Inconvenient Bride – crossover with A
Highland Feuding series!
Related stories (same clan 500 years later)
The Earl's Secret
Blame It On The Mistletoe in ONE CANDLELIT
CHRISTMAS

STAND-ALONE STORIES:
The Queen's Man
The Duchess's Next Husband
The Maid of Lorne
Kidnapping the Laird (short story)
What The Duchess Wants – for newsletter
subscribers only!
Upon A Misty Skye
Across A Windswept Isle
A Traitor's Heart in BRANDYWINE BRIDES
The Storyteller – A Ghosts of Culloden Moor (novella)
An Outlaw's Honor ~ A Midsummer Knights romance
Tempted by Her Viking Enemy
The Highlander's Substitute Wife (HIGHLAND
ALLIANCES series)

The KNIGHTS of BRITTANY Series:
A Night for Her Pleasure (short story)
The Conqueror's Lady
The Mercenary's Bride
His Enemy's Daughter

A Medieval Bride Novella

THE CLAIMING OF

Lady Joanna

TERRI BRISBIN

USA TODAY BESTSELLING AUTHOR

The Claiming of Lady Joanna

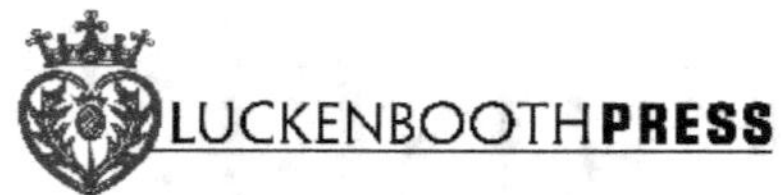

PROLOGUE

Canterbury, England
March, in the Year of Our Lord 1201

He was certain his head would split open if he did not clench his jaws together. Such rage filled him that Braden knew nothing good would come from saying any of the things he was thinking.

The damn girl had refused him!

And she'd done so in front of King John's court. The king was highly amused by her antics, as was his court, but the situation simply added to Braden's dark standing among the nobles of England. Most of those who served the king's interest laughed only because they had his protection. Braden's reputation scared them into better behavior when John was not present.

Why had her parents not obtained her consent before making the matter an issue in public view? Her arguments, articulated before a randy king willing to grant his new wife any request, had resulted in John's declaration that the lady must publicly consent to the match.

Although he found her courage before her parents' and his rage and the king's scrutiny somewhat admirable, she needed to be brought to heel quickly and firmly and he was the one who could do it. Even though his plans for her were not as black as some who believed his family's sordid past would suggest, he would not suffer such an insult without retribution and punishment against the one responsible. And Lady Joanna was that guilty soul.

God help her.

When he thought he might be able to speak without revealing the extent of his rage, he turned back to face the unhappy couple who did stand before him. They had the sense to realize how angry he was and what they stood to lose if their daughter did not go through with their arrangements. They wanted this marriage for their own reasons, as did he. They would have to make this right.

"The betrothal is completed, with or without her approval. But, I must have her consent at the wedding ceremony."

"Aye, my lord," Joanna's father stammered out. Everyone there at the king's Easter court knew of his decision now.

"Bring her to me at Wynwydd by the end of the month and make certain that only words of acceptance and consent come out of her mouth. I will handle the matter if you do not, but our agreement will change, as well."

Lord Robert turned to his wife and dismissed her with a wave. When they were alone, Joanna's father spoke again.

"She will give her consent to anything you ask, my lord. I promise you that. Worry not, my lord. She will give it at Wynwydd."

If Braden had misgivings about any harsh treatment his betrothed would receive at the hands of her parents, he banished them quickly from his thoughts. The girl could do with some days of bread and water and a few days on her knees in prayer—the most frequent methods of convincing a wayward girl to follow the wisdom and wishes of her parents.

"At Wynwydd, by month's end," he said, nodding to the other man.

"And the gold, my lord?" Lord Robert's unease at asking was clear; his hands shook, and he would not meet Braden's gaze.

"The agreement was gold for a wife. When I have a wife in name and truth, you will have your gold. And not before."

"She will comply, my lord," Lord Robert answered with confidence now. "Just leave her to me."

Lord Robert bowed and backed out of the room, leaving Braden alone with his anger. He needed a wife and the lord of Blackburn needed gold to rebuild his fortune and his lands. An acceptable trade for both parties. This had to work.

Braden walked to the table and poured a goblet full of the rich, red wine served by the king. Drinking it down without pause, he tried to allow his anger to pass. The girl would be brought to him at his estate near Wales within a few weeks. She would give her consent and they would marry. Her parents would receive their payment. The rumors whispered about the warlock lords of Wynwydd who killed the wives and servants who displeased them would be silenced. And his name, threatened with extinction, would continue.

All would be well.

It had to be.

ONE

Welsh Marches
April, in the Year of Our Lord 1201

"Cut it."

"But, my lady…"

"You must do this for me, Enyd. I fear that my hands shake too fiercely and I would take off my ear as well as my hair."

Joanna's attempt to calm her maid through humor did not work. Although Enyd held the shears closer now, the look of refusal on her face did not change.

"'Tis never been cut, my lady. Not since you were a wee one," Enyd said, drifting off into her thoughts. "Is there no other way?"

The waves of pain returned and Joanna fought against the weakness. She had so little time. The journey to Wynwydd would take only a day longer and then her fate was sealed. After finally succumbing to the beatings, she'd given her parents the words they wanted to hear. As the intensity and frequency of the lashings had increased, Joanna knew that her stubbornness and continued refusal to consent to the marriage would get her killed.

Well, if she had to die, at least she would choose the time and place, and it was not in the clutches of a warlock who would lay a curse on her soul even as she went to her death. 'Twould be in Scotland, with her sister.

Her hand slid up to her cheek and she felt the rising heat there. Time was slipping away and the small party of holy brothers traveling north to their home would be leaving just after dawn. The herbal concoction given to her to keep away fever was not working. From the sticky feeling that trickled down her leg, she knew that one or more of the wounds had reopened and were bleeding again.

"Enyd, if you love me, you will do this now, and then be gone. If you know not of my plans, my parents cannot hold you responsible." Or torture it out of her.

Tears poured down the old woman's cheeks as she raised the shears and cut off ten-and-eight years of growth that lay over her shoulder in one braid. Joanna closed her eyes as the sharp blades chopped through her hair. Swallowing against the pain, she waited for the servant to finish. Enyd stood with the long, dark braid in her hands and shook her head.

"A lady's crowning glory," she murmured sadly as she held it out to Joanna.

That glory was difficult to mask and her disguise would be the difference between escape and death. After a moment of mourning for all that should have been otherwise in her life, Joanna nodded to the woman who had cared for her for as long as she could remember a caring face and voice.

Enyd threw her arms around Joanna and the searing pain of the embrace made her hiss. Not willing to miss the moment, she held on tightly and breathed in the woman's comfort for as long as she could endure it. Then, releasing her, Joanna stepped back and nodded at the door of the chamber. Without another word, Enyd left and Joanna struggled to gather what she needed for the journey ahead.

She had bartered a bracelet for clothing and some small coins that would draw less attention. Pulling the bundle out from under the bedcovers, she made quick work of removing her gown and tunic. She tugged up the longer stockings over her own and tied them to the belt for that purpose. Joanna took her extra chemise from her traveling trunk and tore it into strips. Then she bound her breasts down as flat as she could manage. For once, not being well-endowed was a blessing.

Replacing the bandages on the back of her legs took a few minutes and she also listened while she worked, worrying that the rest of her party was rousing for the day. Balancing herself on one foot then the other, she tied on the leather shoes. Finally, she tossed whatever additional pieces of clothing and jewelry she could find into the sack she'd obtained in her trade and pulled the hood that lay around her neck up as far as she could to cover her face.

Looking around the room for anything left behind or anything that would give away her plans, she realized that she had nothing here. Joanna knew that she should feel some guilt over what she was doing—any God-fearing woman would. But the thought of escaping the imminent death her marriage would mean and making a life with her sister in Scotland gave her a moment of hope. Her parents, who had left her on her own so much, would have to fend off the warlock of Wynwydd by themselves.

Now more servant than lady in appearance, Joanna hunched down and walked toward the back stairs of the inn. Passing a few serving women already beginning their tasks for the day, she mumbled greetings in return for theirs. A few minutes of wending through the darkened corridors of the building and she pushed the door open and stepped out into the yard.

Spring was truly progressing through the English countryside. The smells of the blossoming trees that surrounded the inn and the roads filled the air with their sweet aromas. The warbling of the birds of dawn—sparrow, robin and lark—greeted her as she made her way through the crowded work area toward the resting place of the monks of Holme Cultram Abbey. Sweat beaded Joanna's upper lip and trickled down her neck and face.

She must make it to them before the fever took control. Whispering a prayer to the Almighty that they would take an ill stranger on their journey, she found them already preparing for the road ahead.

"Good brother," she said, greeting the apparent leader of the group in a voice as deep as she could force it. "I was told that travelers could seek safe passage with you on your journey north?" She fought the urge to adjust her hood as she felt the scrutiny of the monk passing over her.

"We welcome the company of anyone sent to us by the good Lord, my son. Join us and may the miles ahead pass quickly as prayers to His Glory." The monk pointed to a place among the others.

Joanna mumbled a reply and followed the gesture until she was behind one of the other monks in the party. In a few minutes, the whole group was making its way along the well-rutted road, walking a few paces behind a cart that carried the oldest and ill disposed of their group. Large enough to offer some protection, but not large enough to draw undue attention, she allowed herself to dream of success.

The road and the trees blurred together and she soon struggled for every step she took. Chills passed in waves over her, making her shiver in spite of the layers of clothing and the exertion of the pace. Then, heat grew in her head and limbs and threatened to overwhelm her. When one of the older monks approached her with questions about her condition, the world around her grew dark and she felt herself falling to the ground.

The days and nights melded together and she had no idea of how many had passed when she returned to herself at last. In spite of the layers of padding beneath her body, she ached as the small wagon in which she lay hit every bump and rut in the rough road. Her groans brought the attention of the cart's driver, a wizened old man whose blue eyes still blazed with life's forces.

"Ye are still with us? I feared we'd be digging yer grave on our arrival at the abbey."

Joanna felt her clothes and found her hood around her neck. Pulling it up on her head, she leaned up on her elbows to look around. She tried to speak, but her throat was sore from being ill and lack of water. The driver held out a skin to her and she took it, anxious to ease the burning.

"Here now, have a care. Too much and ye will just heave it up."

Joanna nodded and took a smaller amount than she wanted. After it slid down her throat and settled in her stomach, she took another sip. The man smiled a near-toothless grin as she heeded his warning. She handed it back to him and tried to sit up. The rocking motion of the cart and the soreness of her body kept her from doing it.

"Rest a bit more. The good brother who has cared for ye said ye are lucky to be among the living after that fever nearly took ye."

So, the fever had gotten worse. And the monks had taken over her care. Had they discovered her secrets, as well? When she would have pursued the matter, exhaustion struck her and she found herself drifting off to sleep again. She needed to know so much—where they were, when they would arrive at the abbey, where she could seek safe haven.

None of that mattered as sleep overtook her once more.

Two

Joanna of Blackburn had best be dead when he caught up to her.

Braden rubbed the rain from his face for the tenth time in only a few minutes and searched through the torrents for some sign of the promised haven. His men slowed with him as they cautiously followed the muddy path. Surely the monks' directions were accurate? They should have reached Silloth Keep hours ago.

One of his men called out and pointed in the distance. A large, dark stone fortress stood to the west of them, and only a flash of lightning had revealed its presence and now led the way. They reached it and approached the gates. Guards called out from one of the towers to challenge their entry.

"Who goes there? State your name and your business," called one of the guards.

"I am Lord Braden of Wynwydd and seek the hospitality of Lord Orrick for the night," he answered. "Brother Lawrence sent me."

The brother's name eased his way, for the gates began

to open in spite of the hour and the growing darkness. A soldier walked forward to meet them and directed them to the entrance to the hall. A few boys took their mounts and Braden climbed the steps to where the guard said the great hall of the keep, and his lord, was. As he entered the large room, he noticed a guard had gone ahead of them to inform his lord of their arrival. Braden and his men waited for a sign of their welcome here.

"Lord Braden, come and join us in our meal," a man he assumed was Lord Orrick called out. "Warm yourself here before the fire."

Braden nodded and strode to the dais and around the high table to where Lord Orrick stood. He noticed his men being directed by a servant to a table just in front of the steps. They would remain in his sight and close enough to come to his aid if needed. As he stopped before Lord Orrick, his stomach let out a loud growl, probably encouraged by the aromas of a steaming pot of stew and the hot loaves of bread on the table.

"Share our meal first, my lord, then we can see to your other comforts," the woman to Lord Orrick's right said. His wife?

"I am Orrick of Silloth and this is my ladywife, Margaret."

"I am Braden of Wynwydd," he replied, holding out his hand in greeting. Orrick grasped his forearm and Braden returned the gesture. Both men were unarmed. "My thanks for your offer of hospitality this night."

He moved to the chair indicated at Lady Margaret's side and was impressed by the prompt and thorough attention he received. A servant helped him remove his dripping wet cloak and gloves. In spite of the meal already being in progress, a laver bowl appeared to his right as soon as he was seated and then a towel so that he could wash.

The fare was hearty, well-cooked and seasoned and Braden listened to the banter between Lord Orrick and his retainers. The ease of exchange and conversation told him much about the way that Orrick managed his manor and his people.

"So, tell us, Lord Braden, what is the news from court?" Lady Margaret asked him as honey-coated cakes and other treats were served along with cheeses and wafers as the last course.

"The king held his Easter court at Canterbury and the queen joined him there." All of England knew about the scandalous marriage of John to Isabella of Angouleme. "Their plans to leave for Normandy were in place even before the holy day was observed."

"Is there trouble in Normandy?" the lady asked. "I would have expected them to stay in England through the summer."

"None that was the subject of open discussion, but some old wounds have not healed."

He probably should have guarded his words. The Lusignans' claim to prior betrothal was known throughout the continent and England. However, the ties to that family were not so strong here. From the comments overheard at the abbey, Lord Orrick kept to himself and had not ventured to court in over a score of years.

The lord and lady exchanged knowing glances. So, their lack of attendance on the king did not mean a lack of knowledge of the maneuverings of the Plantagenet kings.

"What brings you to this part of England, Lord Braden?" Lord Orrick asked in a quiet voice that managed not to draw the attention of anyone except his wife. The lady missed nothing that happened between them.

"I would speak to you in private, if I may. 'Tis a personal matter," Braden answered as he fought the urge to grit his teeth again.

He hated that he would have to reveal, to this stranger, his betrothed's refusal to marry. He despised showing weakness, but Joanna's actions necessitated this and many other humiliations to him. Before he could say anything else, Lady Margaret intervened.

"My lord, our guest has still not shaken off the chill of the road. Can this not wait until morn?"

"Of course, my lady." Orrick nodded to his wife first, then to him. "Join me after you break your fast in the morn, Lord Braden." Orrick stood and held out his hand to his wife. "My steward will see to your comfort and to that of your men."

If the haste with which the lord and lady left the hall was unseemly, no one but he took notice of it. Within moments, Orrick and his very fair wife were gone. Orrick's steward approached him with instructions on the sleeping arrangements and surprised Braden with the offer of a private chamber. Grabbing up a few of the apples, he took them with him as he left the dais to speak to his men.

Remembering the cautious steps of his horse on their approach to the keep, he decided to check it in the stables before retiring. His men, assured of food and ale and a challenging dice game, were well cared for. As he walked through the hall and out into the yard, a pang of wanting, so strong that it took his breath away, struck him. Looking around he knew that this was what he wanted—a well-ordered, successful estate, his people well fed, and a family to enjoy it with him. Pushing away such sentimental thoughts, Braden focused on his problem.

First, he needed to find his betrothed and take her to Wynwydd. Then he needed to show his people that he could keep a wife and gain an heir. The wise-woman of his village had assured him that a spring bride, a woman of black she said, would be fruitful.

His initial reaction was to scoff at the instructions she'd given him; any logical man would have. The ceremony should take place outside the walls of his castle, away from any place of death or fear and under a bower of fresh flowers and blossoms and vines. He should plant his seed during the time of the earth's own fertility, in that same bower, and the dew of his wife's release should mix with the morning dew. Gwanwyn promised that his seed would grow and produce a son and end the curse that had haunted their family for the past five generations.

So, after years of not believing the stories and living in a sort of cowardly refusal to seek a wife and sons, Braden had finally faced the need for an heir. And he did not want to follow in the steps of the other Wynwydds before him—he wanted to live and see his sons. The wise-woman, raised in the ancient Cymric traditions, had been his last hope.

Braden strode down the path that led to the stables. Shaking his head, he laughed under his breath at the speculation and rumors about his family and the powers they supposedly had. Although they were suspected of being warlocks and able to lay curses on others, it was someone else's words that had seemed to damn the Wynwydd males to never living long enough to see their sons.

All the deaths or injuries seemed to be natural, no foul play evident, but none of his male relatives or ancestors back to his great-great-great-grandfather had ever looked on a living son. Even wives were not immune from it— many had died while birthing sons who did not survive. The birth of daughters had saved many a Wynwydd life, but sons had been costly to produce and never enjoyed.

By the time a son was born, his father had either died or gone mad or was blind. A terrible legacy and one which he prayed he'd found a way to end.

Braden arrived at the stables and knew, from the quiet surrounding it, that all grooming and care was done for the night. Seeking the door, he opened it slowly and quietly so as to not disturb the animals inside and let his eyes adjust to the darkness. His horses stood in the stalls closest to this doorway and he found and quieted his own mount with a few soft whispers and an apple from Orrick's table.

It took but a few moments to check the horse's back leg and determine that there was no injury. As he closed the gate of the stall behind him, a soft sound caught his attention. Turning around and peering down the shadowed line of stalls, he realized it came from the back of the stables. Following the enchanting sound, he walked softly on the packed dirt so as to not disturb the maker of it. A few yards from the back wall, he found the source.

A lantern burned low, giving light to a small circle of the stables. Behind the last stall was an area where someone slept. A few blankets tossed in the corner made up a sleeping pallet, and the lantern and a cup and an empty bowl sat on a wooden crate. Then the crooning began again and he found the person making it, leaning over a colt that lay unmoving in the nearest stall.

He froze as he recognized the voice. He'd stood

behind her at the Mass at court, knowing she was meant for him before she did and wanting no surprises when she was presented to him. Her voice, then raised in the singing of a hymn, was clear and strong and its purity had sent chills through him. Those same chills moved through him now as he listened in wonder as she sang softly to the ill horse. Though softer, there was no mistaking the voice of his betrothed.

Lady Joanna of Blackburn was here in Silloth.

Braden's fists clenched, even as his jaws did, while he watched her tender care for the unfortunate horse. Dressed as a boy with her ankle-length black hair under some filthy hood and her womanly curves beneath a loose tunic and cloak, she soothed the animal. Tempted to step forward and end her farce, he knew he must make plans before claiming her. 'Twould be better, now that he'd found her alive and well, to gather his men, take her and leave this keep just before dawn. Once the gates opened, he could be gone from Silloth and Orrick's lands without ever having to explain his reasons for being here and without risking interference from this local lord.

Convinced of his plan, he waited for her own movements to cover his own and, with a care for silence, Braden walked down the aisle and slipped out of the stables. He returned to the keep and spoke to his men, preparing them to meet him at the stables. The comfortable chamber, with its rope-strung bed and soft mattress, was a waste, for he slept not at all while waiting to spring his trap and catch his bride. When the first rays of light crept into the dark clouds of dawn, he was already dressed and standing next to the stables.

Two of his men soundlessly guided their horses from the stalls and readied them for a quick escape. Another two stood guard at both of the doorways to the stables and one more protected his back as he crept nearer and nearer to the woman who had thwarted him. As everyone took their positions, Braden knelt down at her side and thought on how best to accomplish this without alerting Silloth's lord and guards to his actions.

"Joanna," he whispered into her ear as he straddled her sleeping form. When her eyes flew open and focused on him, he covered her mouth with one hand and encircled her neck with the other. "Say not a word. Make not a sound and you might live through this."

Her quickly indrawn breath and immediate thrashing about told him that she recognized him even in the darkened stables. He grasped her neck tighter and hoped she would realize that her struggles were useless. Fearing that he would hurt her, he leaned closer.

"Cease!" he said harshly. "Come, we must leave now."

One of his men whispered a warning about the village waking for the day and his attention strayed from the woman beneath him for a brief moment. When he turned back to pull her to her feet, he was met with the sharp end of a deadly looking dagger. Before he could stop her, she had shoved the dagger through his tunic and stopped just before reaching the part of him that would be needed to make sons.

"Truly, lady, you task my patience. Once we arrive in Wynwydd, I will show you what such behavior will cost you."

Their stalemate surely lasted for an eternity—he did not move his hands, or any other part of him, and she kept a firm pressure against the blade. Finally, he gathered his thoughts together and squeezed her throat harder for a second. As she reacted to it, he rolled quickly from her, letting go of her mouth and neck and grabbing for the dagger. Twisting her arm and hand until she released her grasp on it, he flung it as far as he could. Climbing to his feet, Braden dragged her with him. When they stood, his man retrieved the dagger and held it out to him.

"I wish not to gag you and truss you up like a goose for the table, but will if need be." He watched as she staggered to her feet, leaned over and braced her hands on her knees and gasped for breath. "If Lord Orrick's people are alerted, some may be harmed. I certainly need no more sins marking my black soul. Do you wish to add to your burden?"

Her dark eyes widened once more, and he thought she would answer. Her mouth, now swollen from his hand, worked, but no sounds came out. She touched her throat and neck and he saw the bruises under the layer of dirt she wore now. When she stopped gasping, and when Braden was certain he had her compliance, he wrapped his hand around her arm and led her from the stables.

"Lord Braden? Would you like to explain why you abuse my hospitality and seem intent on stealing my stable boy?" Lord Orrick stood blocking his path and a large number of heavily armed soldiers surrounded the stables.

Braden would never know what made him do what he did next. He could blame it on desperation or a need to avenge his humiliation or just simple rage, but some devil sat on his shoulder goading him. Lifting the dagger still in his hand, he turned Joanna toward him, placed the tip of the blade under her tunic and, with one powerful stroke upward, sliced through the layers of clothing on her. He tossed the dagger to one of his men and took her by the shoulders and turned her to face Lord Orrick.

"This, my lord, is not one of your stable boys. This is my betrothed, Lady Joanna of Blackburn."

THREE

Lord Orrick looked away from her disgrace. His face was like granite as he nodded to his soldiers, and they followed his lead. The hood she wore to cover her hair and most of her face had slid down onto her shoulders and the strips of linen that bound her breasts fell loose to her waist. She could hear the anger in each breath taken by the man holding her.

Braden of Wynwydd. Her betrothed husband. Master of enchantments and killer of women.

A noise drew her attention and broke the mad spell that held them motionless. The lady of the keep pushed her way through the men in the yard and to her husband's side. After a moment of hesitation to take in the scene before her, Lady Margaret walked directly to Lord Braden, pulled the ties of his cloak and began tugging it from his shoulders.

The lady's actions must have surprised him into reaction, for he stepped back, removed his cloak and tossed it over Joanna's shoulders to cover what he had exposed to all.

"Lord Braden, if would you join me in the solar, mayhap we can sort through this confusion?" Lord Orrick said in a voice that was tinged in anger. When Lord Orrick's soldiers moved to surround them, she knew it was no polite invitation. Braden nodded and held out his hand to her, but Lord Orrick stopped him. "If you would allow Lady Joanna some time with my wife, she can make herself presentable."

Lord Braden moved closer to her and wrapped his hand once more around her arm so that she could not escape. "With all respect, my lord. I have searched many weeks to find the lady. I do not wish her out of my sight right now."

Her escapade was over. As soon as he took her from these walls, Joanna suspected her life would be ended, too. The fury on her betrothed's face made him fearsome to behold and, in that moment, she believed every wicked and dangerous thing she'd ever heard about him. Joanna could not stop the shudders that moved through her nor the fear that she was sure covered her face as he met her gaze.

Lady Margaret came to her side and spoke to Lord Braden in a soft voice. "My lord, let me see to the lady's condition. She has lived as you see her since she sought sanctuary here nigh on to a fortnight ago."

The rest of the words blurred in her thoughts, the only one that she heard, that repeated over and over was sanctuary. She'd found it here in Silloth. Lord Orrick had accepted her story and given her a place to heal and to rest. She knew that it had been a temporary one and that she could not stay here, but for the few nights, she'd felt safe here.

Now, Lord Braden's arrival had crushed her plans.

"—sanctuary," Lady Margaret said.

Shaking her head, Joanna realized she'd missed the rest of the lady's words, but the searching look in the lady's eyes told her that it was a message. Confused and frightened, Joanna listened more carefully. She began to walk again and felt the soft touch of the lady at her side. Meeting her eyes, Joanna watched her mouth the word again—sanctuary.

The meaning finally struck her and she stumbled as she realized it. The family chapel had just been enlarged and rededicated, and it was a short distance away. A man could claim sanctuary in a church for forty days, more if supported by the bishop. Did she dare? Could she gain sanctuary and then wait out Lord Braden and his interest in her? Could she dare not to try?

His grip loosened as she stumbled again trying to keep up with his long strides. Taking advantage of his inattention, as she had in the stables, Joanna tore free and sprinted down the path that led to the stone building some yards away. It must have been shock that held everyone else in their places as the distance between her and her betrothed increased. The loud roar signaled an end to that period of grace.

Any advantage her knowledge of the layout of Silloth gave her, the slippery mud left after the storms of the last day took away. Sliding around one corner and then almost losing her balance, Joanna saw the stone chapel surrounded by the low fence ahead. Dropping Lord Braden's cloak as she labored to keep up her pace, she could hear him and his men catching up to her. Jumping the fence, she pushed open the door and ran to the altar. Father Bernard was preparing for Mass and, tugging her hood back up and her disheveled clothing back together, she grabbed for the edge of his robes.

"Sanctuary, Father," she choked out. "I beg sanctuary."

He looked bewildered and then nodded, a serious expression on his face. "Of course, my son. Sanctuary is granted. What matter can be so grievous that you must seek refuge in God's house?"

The crash of the door behind her, the loud swearing and entrance of Lord Braden, Lord Orrick and the others gave him an answer.

"The evil lord of Wynwydd, Father," she whispered without looking at his approach, hesitant to call him a warlock in his hearing. "My life, my very soul, is in danger if he takes me from here."

The priest stuttered and stumbled back as Joanna found herself lifted from her knees and thrown over Lord Braden's shoulder. She pounded on his back as he walked to the door of the chapel, obviously intent on taking her. Then, when she thought all was lost, their progress was halted.

"Father, did you grant sanctuary?" Lord Orrick called out. Twisting around, she could see that he blocked the doorway, backed by a full contingent of his guards.

Father Bernard ran to the door and sidestepped to get around Lord Braden. Glad that she could not see Lord Braden's face, she was nonetheless certain it was darkened by rage. 'Twas then that she realized she'd never seen him smile. What would his face look like if it was lightened by a smile? It must be hanging upside down over a warlock's back that caused such strange and wayward thoughts in her.

"I did, Lord Orrick. This man—"

"This woman. This is a woman, Father," Braden growled as he slid her to her feet. Pulling the hood from her head, he repeated his claim, "This is my betrothed wife, Lady Joanna of Blackburn, and you cannot grant her sanctuary here. I speak for her, and she will accompany me back to my estates now. Besides, women are not entitled to seek refuge in a church."

Still dizzy from being carried in such a manner, she swore she saw a look of pity on Lord Orrick's face. Strange. It seemed to be directed at Lord Braden and not at her.

"You would interfere with me taking custody of the woman given in betrothal to me before the king himself? Lord Orrick, you draw yourself into a battle in which you need not participate." Lord Braden's voice bristled with frustration.

The lord of Silloth seemed to hesitate at the mention of the king, but only until his wife reached his side. Her presence appeared to give him a stronger resolve in his actions. Lady Margaret slipped her smaller hand into her husband's larger one. Could Joanna be safe?

"The soul before us has asked for refuge in God's house, my lord. Unless Father Bernard rescinds his words, sanctuary has been declared and we have no choice but to honor it."

"If I cannot take her from this place, then neither can she leave until we resolve this matter. My men will stand guard at the door to ensure the lady's safety," Braden said.

Joanna nearly smiled at the blatant insult to Lord Orrick. She watched the two noblemen parley in low voices as to the arrangements for who would stand guard. Within a few minutes, she was left alone inside the chapel while everyone else, save two guards, followed Lord Orrick back to the keep.

She turned around and around, looking at the interior of the building and realized that, but for the raised wooden altar and a few benches along the back wall, it was empty. Pulling the rough edges of her tunic together and wrapping her arms around her waist, she tried to plan her next step.

Joanna felt his presence once more before even a word

was spoken. She backed away with each step he took toward her, finally stopping when her legs met one of the benches along the wall. He grabbed the tunic she wore and pressed his hard body against hers until she could feel the heat of him seeping into her. With but one finger under her chin, he forced her head back so that her eyes met his.

His eyes were the color of the greens of spring. Deep and clear, they reminded her of the creeping ivy that clung to the side of this very building and of the newly sprouted leaves on the tall oak trees of the forest. But if his eyes were of spring, his mouth and the kiss he gave were of the summer's scorching heat.

Nothing in her life until this time prepared her for the claiming of his mouth on hers. The polite kiss exchanged during their betrothal was nothing, nothing, when compared to this one. The fury he felt was there, as was something else she could not identify. He pressed his lips to hers and she felt the message he gave. She gasped as his hand slid to her waist and inside her torn tunic and he used her surprise to enter her mouth with his tongue.

Over and over he tasted her and he pushed inside with his tongue again and again until she offered hers to him. A grunt answered her surrender and he suckled on hers even as his fingers teased the sensitive undersides of her now-unbound breasts. When she would have protested, he delved deeper into her mouth and now held her head in one of his hands, not allowing her to pull away.

If she could.

If she wanted to, which she doubted at that moment.

"This is God's house, my lord," the priest said with a cough.

Lord Braden did lift his head now and their gazes met and held. He dipped lower once more and this kiss was more devastating and confusing than the ones given, or taken, before. The barest of touches, a soft moving of his lips on hers, and it was over.

"You are mine, Joanna, by word and pledge, before God and king. And you will be mine, body and soul. Think not that it ends here. This is only the beginning."

His voice was deep and spoke to something within her that she could not understand. In her life, no one had ever wanted her before, so this public claiming of her, even as a possession, made her wonder about things she'd never thought of before. Why did he not simply wash his hands of her? He would lose nothing; her parents, and she, stood to lose everything.

Lord Braden stepped back and she could only watch him leave, the actions and emotions of the past half hour's time finally catching up with her and making her excessively weary and sore. As he strode out the door, she realized that he had once again wrapped her in his cloak.

Gathering it around her, she sought out one of the benches and sat on it. Pulling her legs up within the cloak's thick layers and turning so that most of her weight was not on the backs of her thighs, she leaned back against the wall and sank into the exhaustion that threatened.

Giving up on any comfort to be gained with sitting, she slid down and pulled the wrap around and over her so that only her face was open to the chill of the stone chapel. Sleep claimed her even as she thought on the possessive kiss given, or taken, by the lord of Wynwydd.

"My lord, I appreciate not your interference in this private matter," Braden told the lord of Silloth straightaway. "'Tis a lawful betrothal and I have the papers to prove it."

Braden reached inside his tunic and pulled out the packet of parchments. Orrick took the packet, walked to a table in the room and unfolded them. As the agreements and sworn statements were being examined, Braden tried not to think on his two errors in judgment and actions earlier.

The rage inside him drove him to do such stupid things. He'd been told that it was part of his legacy. All the Wynwydd males were hot tempered…and hot-blooded. What good did it do them to rage against their fate? The futility of the anger forced his hand in situations when calm and cool-headedness would be advantageous.

And what good was the drive to procreate when it meant your own death? Even if he followed the somewhat ludicrous instructions given him by Gwanwyn, there was no guarantee that he would be any more successful in his quest to end the curse that plagued his family. The kiss, and her passionate yet innocent response, just made it worse. Now the need to possess her was greater than before. He wanted to taste her mouth as she screamed out her satisfaction. He wanted to peel off…

Orrick finished reading the documents, stood back from the table and nodded to his wife, who sat in a tall-backed chair near the hearth. So, he was convinced of the legalities. Now Braden could take Joanna and get out of here. Braden cleared his throat.

"You see that I have the right to her?" He placed his fists on his hips. "She is my betrothed and she gave her consent before witnesses to the marriage."

"So it would appear," Orrick said as he rolled the parchments and held them out. "But there is still the matter of sanctuary asked and given in my chapel. 'Tis a serious issue."

"Now that you are content in my rights to the lady, simply give leave to your priest to rescind it."

Father Bernard harrumphed behind him and Braden turned to face him. "Obviously, good Father, you granted the request without knowing the details. Now that you do, you can see that no sanctuary is needed. The lady's lawfully betrothed husband has arrived to escort her home."

"I am bound by the Church's rules on this, my lord. I granted sanctuary before witnesses. To rescind it, I would need the permission of my bishop." The priest stepped closer to Orrick and then spoke again. "If 'tis your will, Lord Orrick, I will begin my petition now to the bishop of Carlisle to release the bond of sanctuary given."

The priest was dismissed with one look from Orrick and no one spoke until the door closed behind them, leaving only the three of them to talk.

"Lord Braden, I would prefer not to involve the bishop in this, for the bishop's attention might gain the king's, as well. Can we not handle this quietly?" Orrick walked to where his wife sat and touched her shoulder. "Allow my wife to speak to Joanna and mayhap this can be worked out with little further trouble?"

Obviously, the lord of Silloth did not want the attention of the king? What was at work here in this seemingly sleepy corner of England? Well, if he spoke the truth, he wanted no more scrutiny of any kind on this matter—the humiliation of her refusal at court still stung and even the document citing her consent given before witnesses did not lessen that. Bringing in the bishop would complicate this and make him a laughingstock in the north as well as the south. He reached up and rubbed his forehead trying to ease the pain that throbbed there.

"Fine. I also do not wish this private matter to draw more attention than it already has. Lady Margaret, please speak to Joanna and discover her requirements for leaving the chapel without resistance."

"Do you know why she is here, my lord? Have you knowledge of her reasons for seeking a safe haven far from home?"

The lady's voice was soft, but the accusing tone in it gave him pause. Other than exchanging their vows at the betrothal, he'd not spoken directly to her…ever. All correspondence, arrangements and discussions went through her father, as was appropriate.

"No explanation was given to me, my lady. She disappeared from her parents' care on their journey to my home and they contacted me to aid their efforts in finding her. 'Tis all I know."

A look given by the lady to her lord made him think. Why had she refused him? Why had she run? Did the reasons make it right? Should she not have come to him? A creeping sense of discomfort filled him. Although his family's history was never mentioned, he knew that Lord Robert was aware of the rumors. If nothing else, the amount of gold offered for the shrewd man's daughter would have been a clue. He'd never given it a thought and had allowed his anger and desperation to direct his efforts in tracking and finding her.

"I would see to her comfort, as well, my lord." The

lady's words were to her husband and Orrick looked to him for an answer.

"With your permission, Lord Braden."

"'Tis well. But I would advise not expending too much effort, for my plan is to leave here by midday. I will see to her needs on our journey."

"My lord, would you send Wenda to me?" Lady Margaret stood and approached the doorway.

Braden was confused and intrigued. "Who is this Wenda? A seamstress?" Joanna was wearing the rags of a peasant when he'd found her and the need for proper clothing should be seen to immediately. The smell of the stables permeated her tunic.

"Wenda is a healer, my lord. The lady was just recovering from some illness when the brothers brought her here," Orrick explained. Orrick nodded in answer to his wife and she left.

"Ill?" he asked. The pain in his head increased as he thought of a sick noblewoman in disguise traveling the length of England with no protection. His noblewoman. "What was the cause of her illness?" He turned back to face Orrick.

"I am sure that between Wenda and my ladywife, they will find out the details."

With a nod from her husband, Lady Margaret was gone. 'Twas then that Braden realized that Orrick had known the stableboy was no boy.

"You knew from the time she arrived, did you not?"

"I knew she was not the role she played. The brothers who brought her here told me that much. When she said she sought work in the stables, I assigned her there."

"You did not think to interrogate her? To discover the truth about her?" Braden fought against clenching his teeth.

"'Tis not my way, Lord Braden. The brothers who brought her knew that she would be safe here until her truth was revealed."

Braden shook his head in disbelief. His betrothed had been allowed to keep her identity secret and work in the stables, all the while the lord of the keep stood aside uninterested in the truth.

"Not your way? Your pardon, Lord Orrick, but how would you know if you were harboring a criminal or a runaway serf? Is it your practice to offer haven to anyone who asks for it?"

"If they come by way of the good brothers, Aye. If I think that a short respite here will give them the strength to continue their journey, Aye. If they—" Orrick hesitated as though thinking over his answer now. "Aye." He crossed his arms over his chest. "Aye, I do."

Braden stopped the angry retort that tried to escape. What a strange place this was and what a peculiar lord who would admit to such a thing! Somehow, though, Braden knew that this place was safe. That if his betrothed had ended up elsewhere, many dire things could have happened to her. That other noblemen would have closed their gates to strangers regardless of the cost of that refusal.

"My thanks."

The words escaped without warning for 'twas not what he wanted to say. Well, mayhap he did? His life had been turned upside down since he let himself believe that Gwanwyn had the answer. He'd bartered for a bride, faced embarrassment before the king and court and ridden the breadth and length of England. With less than a month left in the spring, he knew he must conclude this or it could be the end of his name.

Joanna fit the descriptions given by the Welshwoman—both her coloring and her name were "of black." Something deep inside him spoke of the rightness of this match. Not of the ease of accomplishing it or the difficulty. But, in that place deep within where he allowed himself a measure of ridiculous hope, Braden knew that he needed and wanted Joanna of Blackburn for his wife.

'Twas simply too bad if she did not want the same thing. Too many lives had been lost and generations had perished for a thing like her virginal fears or fancies to matter.

"We could break our fast in the hall while waiting for Margaret's return," Orrick said.

His stomach rumbled its own answer. Braden nodded and waited for Orrick to lead. With his own men guarding the chapel, he knew there was time to eat.

FOUR

"Lady Joanna?"

The sound persisted, but she tried to pay no heed to it. She was so tired and cold and she simply wanted to sleep.

"Lady?"

Now a shake of her shoulder accompanied the voice, making it impossible to ignore. Without loosening the tight cocoon she'd finally made of the overlarge cloak, she opened her eyes and looked around. Lady Margaret stood before her, along with a maid and an old woman who Joanna had seen in the village before.

"So, 'tis true then? You are Joanna of Blackburn?"

"Aye, Lady Margaret," she said, pushing the cloak away and sitting up. Wincing against the pain, she sat upright and faced the lady of Silloth. When she tried to stand, dizziness forced her back down to the bench. "Forgive me, my lady. I am not feeling well."

Lady Margaret clucked her tongue and moved aside for the old woman. The woman reached for the cloak and Joanna instinctively clutched it. Shaking her head, she realized that her disguise, effective for weeks, was useless to her now.

"This is Wenda, our healer. If you will allow her to see to your injuries, she can ease your pain."

Joanna nodded and permitted the old woman to poke and prod her face and neck, shoulders and arms, even stomach and knees. So many places hurt now, she could not pick them out.

"Did he beat you in the stables?"

"Beat me? Nay. But he pounced on me while I was sleeping, twisted my arm to take my dagger and threw me over his shoulders. I ache in so many places from just that."

Lady Margaret and the healer exchanged looks of horror and Joanna realized that her description of Lord Braden's treatment of her sounded very bad indeed. His actions in subduing her did not come close to the cruelty of her parents' so she tried to explain. "And he kissed me."

An expression she could only describe as "stunned" filled their faces and Lady Margaret waved her maid over closer as she and Wenda stepped away. Without a word, the servant poured hot water out of a jug she carried and into a bowl. Producing a small bar of soap and cloth, she proceeded to help Joanna wash her face and neck and hands.

The feel of the heat after so long without washing soothed her and being able to cleanse herself of the layers of dirt was a relief. The whispering between the other two continued until she finished her ablutions, and then they turned back to her. The maid was dismissed with a look and the chapel was silent until they were alone and the door closed.

"I hesitate to ask you this, Lady Joanna, but I think I must." Lady Margaret's tone was soft and her eyes were filled with concern. She took Joanna's hand in hers and patted it. "Did Lord Braden take you…your virginity…in the stables before my lord Orrick arrived?"

She thought Lord Braden had attacked her and taken her virtue? Joanna shook her head. "No, my lady. He did not…do that."

Another glance between them. Wenda spoke this time. "I think the pain is from some bruises and being roughly handled, my lady. I do not think there are any serious injuries." Wenda stepped away. "Some rest should be all that is needed for that."

"Before you leave, Wenda," the lady began. "Joanna, the brothers who sent you here said that you had been ill through the whole journey. Do you know what caused the fever you suffered?"

So, the good brothers had not examined her during the journey from the south? They had simply treated the fever? Still she hesitated to discuss her parents' treatment of her and their attempts to gain her consent for the marriage. She really did not want to talk about all that had transpired before she'd run away.

"I know not, my lady. Did the brothers have any hint of the reason?" She looked at the lady and waited.

"None that they shared with me, I fear." When it appeared that she would say something else, the lady shook her head instead. "Wenda, we will call you if we have need."

And then they were alone.

"Lord Braden is demanding that you be turned over to him."

Joanna could not help her reaction—the shudder tore through her, making her shake and tremble. Pushing her hair out of her face, she tried to stand once more. This time she gained her feet. "But, I have been granted sanctuary here. Will he ignore the priest's words?"

"Lord Braden is not willing to recognize that, Joanna. He wants to take you from here this day." The lady walked closer to her. "Mayhap if you can tell me the basis for your flight and your hiding here, I can convince him otherwise."

"He paid my father a large amount of gold for my hand in marriage," she said. "Enough that my father would look no further."

"'Tis the way of things."

"My father would not accept my refusal and took all measures he thought necessary to gain my consent." She looked at Lady Margaret. "All measures." The skin on the back of her thighs and her lower back pulsed with its own memory of the punishments she'd endured.

It did not take the lady very long to realize what she meant. Recalcitrant daughters were dealt with swiftly when a marriage that was advantageous to her family was involved. For certain, Joanna was not the first, nor would she be the last, daughter treated as she had been.

"Did Lord Braden order such things to be done to you? Although he seems brutish, he does not seem cruel," the lady said.

"I do not know if he did or not," Joanna said as she paced the back of the chapel. "I know only that he wanted me to wife and wanted me now. My father redoubled his efforts after I spoke out about the betrothal at court. He swore he would not take the chance of losing such wealth over my concerns."

She had not realized how terrible her words of refusal were until the repercussions spread through King John's court. Then the king's attention and involvement simply guaranteed the treatment she'd received.

"Is it that you do not want to marry the lord of Wynwydd because you fear more beatings?"

She had guessed part of it. But the physical pain, as bad as it had been, was not the worst. She feared dying unloved even more than she feared dying. As so far, in this life, she had been loved by no one but her sister.

"The truth about Lord Braden was discussed almost openly at the king's court, my lady. I fear losing my soul more than I fear losing my life. His true nature will rob me of that before he kills me." Her hands and knees shook as she forced the words out. "He is a sorcerer who will curse me even as his family is cursed. 'Tis widely known that Wynwydd wives do not survive."

Silence filled the stone building. 'Twas the first time she'd voiced the fear to anyone save her maid Enyd, but she'd heard the stories every day at court. The fates of Lord Braden's father and grandfather and most male relatives were well-known—they died under mysterious circumstances or went mad. Some said it was caused by trying to control the unworldly powers they'd been given. Some said the Wynwydd males were simply evil incarnate—one only had to look into their eyes to feel the malevolence. Anyone who knew anything agreed she would never live to see the next anniversary of her birth.

"Is this the reason you ran from him and the betrothal? Where will you go if not with him?"

"My sister lives in Scotland. I was trying to reach her when I…became ill. I confess, I was using my time here to regain my strength to make the rest of the journey." Joanna walked closer to the lady. "I am sorry to have brought you into this. Your lord offered me a haven and I have brought the very devil to his doorstep."

Lady Margaret said nothing in reply. Instead, she stared off toward the altar and shook her head. "And now? How would you have this standoff end?"

"If Lord Braden takes me from this keep, he will kill me. I saw it in his eyes when he first took me in the stables. He means to avenge the insult to his honor that he blames on me. Do you think that Lord Orrick will support his priest in this, or will he comply? Will he allow Lord Braden to take me from here?"

"'Tis not Lord Orrick's decision, lady." His deep voice broke into the discussion and shook her to her core. He walked across the small chamber and, in spite of her resolve to face him, Joanna found herself shrinking back, preparing for the worst. "Lord Orrick has no standing in this and neither does his priest. You," he said as he stalked her on the last few steps to the church's wall and pinned her with his nearness and his intense glare, "answer to me and only to me."

He towered over her and she felt the fear flood back into her soul. Mayhap he would kill her quickly if she acquiesced now and caused no more delays. Then, some spark within her flared and she pushed her chin up and met his terrifying countenance. She did not want to die and did not think that the good Lord had watched over her this long to let her perish in His own house.

"My lord, the lady needs some rest. Can you not delay your decision for a day to allow her that?" Lady Margaret actually positioned herself between them, forcing Lord Braden to back away a few steps from her. "I am certain her outlook will improve with rest."

Her betrothed looked from one to the other before replying. A suspicious glint entered his eyes. Did he remember that 'twas Lady Margaret's words that had spurred Joanna to run here?

"Another day will allow the roads to dry from the

rains. I think it a good idea to remain for one more day."

He stressed the last words, unknowingly giving her both an ultimatum and another chance to escape his grasp. If Lady Margaret would assist her, she could sneak out during the night and be miles ahead of him. Lord Braden nodded to Lady Margaret and then began to leave. He paused near the door. "I will escort you back to your husband."

"Is there another way out of here?" Joanna whispered to Lady Margaret when she came closer. "If you can distract his men, I will try to get out of the gates before he knows. I have some food, a few coins and my bag hidden in the stables. It can only be a few more days' journey to my sister's."

"I would urge you to careful consideration of any action you plan, Joanna. Such a move could be more dangerous than you know."

But before Lady Margaret could agree to help her or not, Lord Braden interrupted. "I visited a cathedral in London once that had the most amazing architectural feature." He turned to face them and continued with an ill-timed explanation of his travels. "The church had been built in such a way that all sounds moved up the walls, across the ceiling and down the wall on the other side. 'Twas called a whispering dome."

His focus followed the curve of the roof overhead, and the look of triumph told her the meaning of his words—he'd heard her plea to Lady Margaret for help. Could it be so? He opened the door and called out to his men who surrounded the chapel to double the guard and be prepared for her attempt to escape. He had heard her words.

When he held out his hand for Lady Margaret, Joanna felt some small measure of desperation creeping into her. What could she do now? Lady Margaret nodded to him and left Joanna's side.

"Rest now, Joanna. I will return as soon as I've spoken with my lord husband."

Braden followed Lady Margaret and spoke as he pulled the door closed behind them. "As will I."

His voice was filled with both menace and some kind of promise and made her quiver from head to toe. Deserted once again, Joanna sought the meager comfort that her makeshift pallet offered and tried to pray for a safe outcome.

He was the kind of man who would have drawn women to his side with but an inviting glance. Even at her age, two score and one, his fine figure, dark hair and chiseled features stirred an admiration that might have caused problems were she not completely in love with her husband and nearly old enough to be Lord Braden's mother. Margaret walked at his side trying to sort out her assessment before they reached Orrick.

A few things had become apparent rather quickly in this perplexing situation. Lord Braden was a man accustomed to getting his own way and he used his sordid reputation to scare and bully people around to do his bidding. His reputation was well-known by most of England and feared enough to terrify a young woman into running away from the only security and family she'd known. She was not completely convinced that he deserved the reputation he carried.

Or mayhap he did?

A few times she had caught him watching Joanna when he did not know he was being observed. Anger bordering on rage was clear in his features and his tense stance, but there was something else, a desperate longing for Joanna or what she offered, deep in his expression. He hid it quickly as though he feared someone else seeing it. As though it undermined him in some way. As though the desire for her was dangerous to him.

They walked in silence toward the keep. Then, as if he knew she was judging him and his actions, he stopped and turned to face her. One look at his face, his very handsome face, told her that he did not desire her involvement.

"I would advise you to stay out of what is between Lady Joanna and me." He crossed his arms over his chest and looked down at her. "Pardon my candor, Lady Margaret, but I do not appreciate your interference."

She fought the urge to smile as she felt it tug at the

corners of her mouth. She had faced down men more powerful than him in her life and relished the challenge his insult offered. Margaret knew 'twas probably not a good idea to incite him to more anger, but the memory of the terror that controlled Joanna gave her any permission she sought.

"And I do not appreciate stubborn, thick-skulled men who seek to terrorize young women under my protection."

She crossed her arms in the same manner he had and raised her chin. 'Twasn't a fair argument for she knew all but six people in the keep would leap to her defense if need be. That complete support and sense of safety gave her any courage she needed to speak to him boldly.

"Your behavior and insults are unseemly, lady. Surely your husband would counsel you to a more modest demeanor."

She did laugh then. His words would have hurt a woman who was uncertain of her worth. "'Tis at my lord husband's request that I am here. 'Tis through his tutelage and at his urging that I have learned to be forthright in my words and manners. Mayhap a similar attitude on your part toward your betrothed would have prevented the lady from seeking a safe haven from you?"

She would give him some credit—the grimace that crossed his face as she answered his insult with one of her own spoke of the words being considered in his mind. 'Twas a step at least.

His attention moved over her, and he examined her from the top of her head to the slippers on her feet. This frank and open assessment should have embarrassed her, but she recognized it as one opponent for another. Another step on his part.

Was there any hope for these two?

Margaret did know that Joanna was utterly terrified by Lord Braden. She also recognized that part of that terror was due to the effects of her physical condition and part was due to the outrageous rumors she'd heard, ones she suspected he had partly spread himself to keep his life as private as possible.

Sorcerer? Warlock? The devil incarnate?

Although she could believe that women would whisper it of him in certain situations, Margaret did not believe such tales. When there was ignorance about someone, the courtiers who toadied to royalty created whatever they needed to keep themselves amused. There was probably some seed of truth within the words shared by Joanna, but it had been embellished and had grown beyond any semblance of reality.

Until Joanna saw Braden of Wynwydd as a man, she would never leave the chapel and the sanctuary willingly. Until she could separate the reputation from the man beneath it, there was no hope of happiness. And until Braden could shed the myths that he used to protect his secrets, he would never offer Joanna or any woman what they truly wanted.

With a grunt, Lord Braden offered her his arm again and they walked up the stairs into the keep. Surely Orrick would have words of wisdom to offer in this matter.

"No."

"But, Lord Braden, surely you must agree that some accommodations must be made in this situation."

"No," he repeated. The lady wanted clothing and a set of bedding and even a brazier delivered to the chapel so that Joanna would be comfortable while she stayed there.

"Father Bernard decided that it would be inappropriate for him to remain in his chamber while Lady Joanna is in residence so he will stay here in the keep," Lord Orrick announced.

"Then a maid must attend her," Lady Margaret began.

"No!" he shouted as he clenched his fists and teeth. "These arrangements are unnecessary. The lady will leave with me on the morrow."

Braden suspected that the lord and lady of Silloth were in league with his betrothed to prevent him from taking her. Why else would they become so involved over the plight of a stranger.

"And food? Would you deny her sustenance while she is there?" Lady Margaret challenged.

He did not mean to starve her, truly he did not. Braden struggled to control his temper as he faced his adversaries.

"Please, my lady. I only wish to get back to my own lands and people as soon as is possible. Cozening her in this foolhardy course will only prolong her resistance. Feed her, certainly, but leave the rest and let me deal with her."

He'd thought on the lady's earlier words to him and knew she was correct—he was using fear to try to force Joanna to his will. 'Twas the only way he knew to deal with problems like those she presented. For too long his reputation had protected him and his from the prying eyes and greed of nobles and neighbors. He'd even been responsible for some of the tales told, or rather embellished, about his powers. All in an effort to keep away those who would gawk at his family's misfortunes.

Now, when he needed a bride, his own deeds came back and prevented what should have been a normal occurrence for a nobleman—the procurement of a wife. Braden did terrify Lady Joanna. He had seen it in her eyes and felt it in her uneven breathing as he had held her down in the stables. The trembling of her hands and her chin as she looked on him had told him, also.

"This is all most difficult for me," he admitted without thinking on his words. "I will have her to wife and it seems that her actions leave me no other course but to force her from the chapel and take her to Wynwydd."

"There is always a choice, my lord," the lady said in a soft voice. "'Tis never the easiest one to see, but it is the one that holds the most promise."

Concerned about the doubts that were creeping into his thoughts about Joanna, he knew he must control any sign of weakness over his plans for her. Crossing his arms over his chest, he shook his head at them.

"She is mine and she leaves with me in the morn."

When both looked as though they would argue with his declaration, he turned and left the chamber.

FIVE

The sun's rays danced lightly over her features, revealing freckles he'd not noticed before. The dirt that had obscured her pale cheeks was gone, too. The most striking change was her hair. Where it once had fallen to her ankles in ebony waves, now it barely passed her chin and neck and, without the weight of its previous length, it curled and swirled around her face.

Braden watched from the path as Joanna leaned as far as she could out the door of the chapel without taking the step that would remove her from her haven. She stood with her eyes closed and inhaled deeply, looking so much at peace that it made his chest tighten. One of his men called out to him and the moment was disturbed. Now, a look of fear dropped like a veil over her face, and she backed quickly into church and away from him, slamming the door as though it would stop him.

He walked to the men who served as guards and discovered that, although alone now, many people had visited Lady Joanna since he'd left. Lady Margaret and the healer had returned, as well as an assortment of both ladies and maids. Other than the food he'd given permission for, nothing else had been brought into the chapel.

Braden nodded and walked to the now-closed door and felt the absurd need to knock. He did but entered without waiting for a response. Joanna retreated even farther into the shadows of the chapel. She stopped next to the bench where his cloak lay.

"What were you doing at the door?" he asked. Seeing her reaction to his approach, he stopped and waited for her answer.

"There are no windows in the chapel, my lord," she said, nodding her head in the direction of the walls. Her curls moved as she did it and one fell over her forehead. She shook her head to fling it out of the way. "No way to let the sun in."

Braden turned his head to look around the chamber. True, the only light was from burning candles and a small lantern on the altar. Without a word, he walked back to the door and pulled it open. The midday light flooded in, but the direct rays fell only on the doorstep, where Joanna had stood before he came in.

"And you like the sunshine?" He had always favored the shadows.

"Spring is my favorite season of all, my lord. The sun grows stronger and warms the earth. I like the feel of its light on my face." Her voice softened as she spoke and, as her words echoed those of Gwanwyn's, he felt something in his soul soften toward her.

"It has caused your skin to freckle," he said.

She touched her face and nodded, looking away from his gaze. "My mother informed me how unappealing it is to see them on a lady's skin, my lord."

Unappealing? Far from it. The urge to find out where else she had them grew and he fisted his hands to keep from reaching for her. Those things would have to wait until she was truly his.

"You can enjoy being out in the sunshine during our journey to Wynwydd. Once we travel away from the coast, the rains should lessen a bit." He watched as a shudder moved through her. But he would not relent in this. They would leave on the morrow. He took a step closer and crossed his arms. "And we leave in the morn."

She began to shake her head at him, but he stopped her with a wave of his hand. "Do not think to naysay my order on this, lady. You have reached the end of your disobedience in this matter. On the morrow, you shall leave with me and travel to my home as befits the lady of Wynwydd. I will accept no more arguments from you."

"What do you plan to do to me, my lord? Will your punishments wait until we reach your keep or will I not see that?" Her voice was stronger but still trembled as she asked the impertinent question.

"Punishments?"

"Aye, my lord. You have been quite clear to so many about what you will do to me once you take me from here."

She touched her neck where the imprints of his fingers stood out against her pale skin. "Do you really wonder why I would not want the honor of being your wife?"

Lashed by the insult, he felt the blood pulsing in his temples. Control warred with the instinct to strike out at her, to make her realize that she did not have the protection of someone to keep her from the consequences of her actions and words. Not like Lady Margaret's husband, Orrick, whose lack of supervision encouraged his wife's poor example.

"Do you really wonder why I am angry over your behavior? Every action you have taken since your father agreed to our betrothal has held me up to ridicule and embarrassment. Before the church, before the king and his court, before even these strangers. If I seek retribution against you for it, none will object. 'Tis my right as your betrothed husband to correct your wayward tendencies."

Something flared in her eyes and it startled him. For the first time since they'd met, it was not fear. He watched as the anger he felt was reflected back at him by her stance and by the set of her chin. And by her infinitely kissable lips as she pressed them together in some attempt not to speak out her thoughts.

Anger meant her fear was lessening. Anger was something he was familiar with and with which he could deal. Much better for her to be angry than to be afraid.

"Why did you not simply let me go? Why did you have to find me?" she asked.

"I chose you and you were declared mine. I would have followed you all the way to Scotland and brought you back, Joanna." Her eyes widened at his referral to her flight from him to supposed safety in Scotland and he stepped closer. This time, she stood her ground.

"If you returned and announced to my parents that you found and buried my dead body, you would still have your gold and could find another wife. No one would be the wiser for my escape."

Joanna matched his stance by folding her arms over her chest. The slit edges of her shift and tunic gapped and granted him an enticing glance at the curves of her breasts. He really did want to see if the freckles continued down onto them and so Braden took the last step between them and slid his hands into her hair as he'd been longing to do since he saw her at the door.

"I would. I am not willing to give you up," he said, meeting her gaze. "You are mine."

Braden brought her closer and touched his lips to hers. Joanna's hands covered his but did not stop them as he moved them through her silky locks. As he deepened the kiss and turned her face to meet his, he felt her breathing begin to quicken. When she tentatively touched his tongue with hers, he possessed her mouth as he would soon possess her body.

Easing back from her lips, he nuzzled his way down her chin, over to her ear and then onto her neck. Her soft sighs as he touched the sensitive skin there urged him on to bolder deeds. He touched his tongue to the place where the slope of her breasts began and followed the soft skin down to the now-exposed nipple. Braden felt Joanna's hands move to his chest and grasp at his tunic, but she did not stop him.

Sliding his hands down to her waist, he knelt before her and took one of the tightened buds in his mouth, licking and sucking at it until he felt her legs tremble. Then he moved to the other and soon, her ragged breath echoed through the chamber. Braden kissed the line down the center of her stomach and slid his hands around to caress her bottom when she tensed and pulled from his embrace.

"No," she said, shaking her head. "No."

He stood and watched as she tugged the edges of the tunic together and held them tightly. Her breaths were still uneven and he was pleased that she had been affected by his kisses and by his touch. She might be a virgin and not know the ways of physical love yet, but her body was ready for his as much as his was for hers.

"Consummation is all that is left for us, Joanna. The final step in making you my wife. Our last step." He adjusted his belted hose and tunic to ease the tension against the part of him that urged for that act more than any other at this moment.

"I will not say the words at the church door, my lord. I will recant my consent." She stepped away from him and walked a few paces in the direction of the altar. "I still claim sanctuary here."

Her fear of him had lessened and he had tasted of her innocent passion again, but nothing had changed between them. In the morning, it would take force to remove her from this chapel and that sin would be added to his long list of previous ones.

"So be it, lady. I will take you from here if need be."

"I will not come willingly, my lord."

Nodding at her, Braden turned to leave. Mayhap the loneliness and darkness of the church for the rest of the day and night would give her time to relent. If not, he knew what he had to do.

He had no idea about what to do.

Lord Orrick's invitation to dinner had surprised him. He expected to be seated in the back of the hall, but instead found himself at the lord's table. His men were offered every comfort again as was he. The only strange thing was that the women were missing. Lady Margaret and her ladies were gone from the table. No explanation was offered until the meal was finished and then he knew that his mission was in trouble.

"My ladywife is eating her evening meal in the chapel, Lord Braden," Lord Orrick began.

"As is mine," said Sir Royce, Orrick's chief knight and castellan.

"As is mine," added Sir Richard, the knight who

oversaw Orrick's interests in the salt lathes and monastery properties.

"And mine, I fear," said Sir Hugh, captain of Orrick's guards.

"And mine." The words continued down the length of the womanless table as each of Orrick's knights and retainers reported the same occurrence—all the women were in the chapel.

With Joanna.

This could not be a good thing.

Braden did not realize he'd said the words aloud until the men grunted and nodded in agreement. Two pitchers of wine were placed on the table and quickly shared by all. The men ranged in age from young knights about one score in years to Lord Orrick at just past two score and even older.

"What is their purpose there, my lord?"

"Companionship for Lady Joanna, I am certain," Orrick replied but his expression did not look as though he was certain at all.

"Mischief and mayhem," answered another of the men farther down the table. When all the others nodded or grunted in agreement, he could not tell who had spoken the words.

"I do not understand, Lord Orrick. How is it that you allow your wife such behavior? Should you not exert more control and guidance over her? I tell you candidly that she is not setting a good example of wifely behavior for my betrothed."

Every man to a one at the table stopped and stared at him. Had he gone too far and offered too great an insult to his host? Braden swallowed deeply from his cup before looking at Orrick. When he did meet Orrick's gaze, there was amusement there as well as the benevolence of a teacher for his student.

"My ladywife is my partner, Braden. I trust her implicitly as she trusts me. She strives always for my health and happiness as I strive for hers. Margaret knows that any actions she takes on my behalf, any words spoken by her in my name, any protection extended will be supported by me, as she supports all that I do. It has taken us years and many, many mistakes to come to this point, but it has given me all I could want in life."

Braden could hear the conviction in his words and watched as each of the men at the table nodded in agreement. He shook his head trying to clear his thoughts—this was not the way of things. It sounded as though the wives ruled here and the husbands gave way for them.

"Do not misunderstand my words, Braden," Lord Orrick said to him more quietly. "If the need is there for me to give an order, my ladywife will obey me. In all things. But there are better ways to accomplish what you need to do than by making a battle of it."

"You think this is a battle? One I cannot win?"

Braden had fought many enemies in the past. Strategy and planning were his strengths. One mere woman would be no challenge.

Hell.

This woman was more than a challenge—she was a formidable adversary. She'd already begun to undermine his plans by being something, someone, very different from what he had expected.

Still, any softening in his feelings about her did not change his pressing need. Spring was full upon England and his time was limited. If Gwanwyn was correct, he had only a few more weeks in which to return to his lands with his wife. Braden knew he needed to resolve this quickly. He did not have the luxury of time.

"Do not make it one." Orrick stood. "I must check out the battlements of the keep. Join me."

Braden finished the rest of his wine and stood. He followed Orrick through the keep, up several flights of steps until they reached the roof and battlements of the keep. The strong ocean winds buffeted him as they walked to the edge and looked out over the yard and village. They stood in silence for several minutes and Braden thought about how to answer the questions he knew would be asked.

"I can see the anger and the urgency in your actions. Will you share with me the reason?"

Braden let out a breath of exhaustion and frustration. He'd had no one in his life who could understand his burden. His father had never spoken two coherent words to him before his death. No uncle or male cousin had survived long enough to guide him in the quest to protect the family name. Could Orrick help?

"Do you know my lands, Lord Orrick?"

"Please use my given name. 'Tis another of my eccentric ways." Orrick laughed even as he admitted to it. "Wynwydd sounds Welsh."

"It is. My lands lie at the foot of the mountains that separate England from Wales. I am the last of my line, Orrick."

"Ah, the pressure to marry. I understand that well enough."

"I have my reasons, but I cannot disclose them to you." He was simply not ready to trust a stranger with the story of his family's weaknesses.

"More importantly, have you disclosed them to the lady?"

Braden walked a few paces away and looked over the stone wall to the yard. The chapel where the lady in question sat at this moment was below him.

"Her fears are real, Braden. And they've given her a strange strength to be bold and daring. More than most women, and most men, in her situation. Think on it—she came up with a plan to disguise herself and make her own way to her sister's village in Scotland. And, in spite of an unplanned illness, she nearly made it."

Orrick's tone irritated him.

"She disobeyed her parents. She ran from a legal betrothal. She lied before witnesses. And she has drawn you into it. I would not think to hear such admiration in your voice when you realize the problems she could cause for you."

Orrick's amusement quieted for a moment and then he smiled. "I do admire her, Braden, as I am certain you do if you would only admit it to yourself. I would think that she is exactly the kind of wife that the 'warlock of Wynwydd' would want. One filled with spirit and daring and passion."

He'd heard the rumors. Braden had hoped that they had not traveled this far north. "I am not a warlock, Orrick. Surely you know that." Braden faced the lord of Silloth now and shook his head.

"I know that, you know that, but the lady believes it. And she believed it so strongly that it gave her the courage to run from everyone and everything she knew. Breaking through that fear and gaining her trust will be a formidable task."

"I care not if she fears or trusts me, Orrick. I want only her compliance and obedience." Orrick laughed out now and smacked Braden on the shoulder. He felt no such humor.

"Think on your words this night and mine. If you force her to your side, you will gain a wife. If you ease her fears and bring her willingly to your side, you gain a partner. Which would you rather have?"

"If it were only that easy. There is much you do not know."

"Aye, there always is more to any story. But that is between you and the lady. I would urge you to remember that honey draws more flies than vinegar and cats come to cream."

"I have heard those sayings before, Orrick."

"And you must swear never to tell Margaret that I used them in speaking about how to treat women. But, man to man, you must learn to choose the battles you fight, especially with women. And never risk more than you can afford to lose."

Noisy chatter rose from the yard and Braden looked over the wall to see women spilling from the chapel. The evening meal and womanly talks must be at an end. He needed to seek his rest, as well, for he did not relish what the morrow held for him.

Orrick picked up the lantern he'd brought with them and began walking back to the doorway. When they reached it, Orrick looked back at him before opening it.

"I cannot allow you to force her from the chapel tomorrow." When Braden would have argued with him, Orrick held up his hand to stop him. "I think you will see the wisdom of making it seem to be your choice to stay."

The soft scuffling of feet on the stone floor woke her just

as the light of dawn crept over the walls of Silloth. Father Bernard walked to the altar to prepare for daily Mass. Nodding to her, he went to the small chamber behind the altar and brought out the linens he needed. He set about covering the altar and putting out the crucifix and chalice and plate.

There was still time before he would ring the bell and call the faithful to church. The door was ajar and she lay quietly on the bench and watched as the light grew stronger and stronger. Outside.

Outside, where spring would be bursting forth again today.

Outside, where the people of the village would be preparing their fields and planting the seeds that would become food for them.

Outside, where the sun could warm her skin and the wind could ease her spirit.

Joanna stretched and tried to remember all the words of encouragement from Lady Margaret and her women. Never in her life had she been included in such a gathering. Her mother could never stand her presence, so Joanna spent most of her time with her maid and her sister, until her sister left for her own marriage. To be included in the chatter and gossip of the women of the keep had been a wonderful gift.

Every muscle in her body ached and she took a moment and tried to stretch each one to loosen them before trying to sit or stand. Her ribs were the worst, having borne most of the weight when Lord Braden jumped on her in the stables. Wenda had checked her again before leaving last evening and told her, though bruised, nothing was broken.

As she rubbed against the ache, her body remembered the other ache, the one caused by Lord Braden's hot mouth on her skin and her breasts. The tips of them tingled now as she thought on his strange caresses and kisses and the heat they caused in her. When Lady Rosamunde mentioned something later in the evening about her husband, Sir Gautier, doing something that caused her toes to curl, Joanna feared that her blush gave away that she knew something that could do that.

Lord Braden had done that to her. When his tongue had touched her, Joanna swore her toes had curled. Now, her body pulsed with an awareness that had never been there before. Not before he'd kissed her and touched her and… She must stop these thoughts. Surely they were sinful and not appropriate in this place.

"My lady?" Father Bernard whispered. "'Tis time now."

The priest went to the front corner of the chapel and tugged hard on the rope that hung there. The bell above chimed loudly enough to call those in the keep and the village to church.

Joanna sat up and then stood, still wobbling and not steady on her feet. As she stumbled, someone grasped her arm to help her.

Lord Braden.

"My lady, allow me to be of assistance." He brought his arm around her waist and waited while she gained her balance.

"You come to Mass?" she asked in a whisper as they made their way toward the altar. Did not the devil fear the cross and chalice?

"I admit that I am not as religious as I should be, but I do attend whenever I have the opportunity. There is a small but lovely chapel at Wynwydd."

Stunned by his admission, Joanna stared at him and watched for any signs that he was struggling against the Lord's presence here. A few minutes of close scrutiny revealed nothing save his habit of clenching his jaws.

They took places to one side of the altar and waited for the Mass to start. Joanna remembered that her head was uncovered and felt for the hood that she'd worn these past weeks. "My lord, I must cover my head before Mass begins. Let me get my hood at least," she said, slipping from his side. As she searched the bench where she'd slept, she felt him at her side.

"Wear this, Joanna," he said, placing a hooded cloak over her shoulders. It hid her inappropriate attire completely from view and covered her head at the same time. And it fit perfectly.

"Where did you get this?" she whispered as they walked back to their places.

"I brought it with me. A gift for my betrothed. One I did not have the opportunity to present to you upon your arrival at my home."

The priest rang small gold bells that announced the beginning of the Mass so Joanna could not ask him any more questions. She knew that once the Mass was over, he would try to take her from here and she must collect her thoughts and be ready. He stood close to her and she could smell the scent of the soap he must have used recently. A fresh herbal smell, one probably concocted by Lady Margaret for her guests. Taking in a deep breath of it, she realized how badly she must smell.

Braden caught her and gave her a look of puzzlement. He nodded his head at the altar and she comprehended that he was telling her to turn her attention to the priest. Her breath caught as she watched the dimple appear in his chin. His green eyes sparkled with the merriment of one involved in a prank. For a moment she could almost forget that he meant to force her to his will.

Just as she'd forgotten last evening when his mouth caused such magical feelings in her body and her heart. She had nearly surrendered to him, until he touched the still-new wounds on her bottom and her thighs. It would cost her too much to allow simple lust to break her now. Shifting on her feet, she strengthened her resolve to fight his evil plans for her.

Pulling the cloak more tightly around her shoulders, she moved away from him so that his scent and his nearness and his heat would tempt her no longer. Father Bernard said the final blessing and Mass was over. Although most left the chapel, many stood just outside the fence waiting to see what would happen between them.

Lord Orrick appeared at her side and Lady Margaret stood at his. Joanna held her breath about what was to come. She was not strong enough to fight him physically. Only Lord Orrick could do that and she was not certain that he would. They all looked at Lord Braden.

"I will ask you once more, Lady Joanna, to relinquish your claim of sanctuary and come peacefully from this place with me." His deep voice echoed through the chapel. The calm tone surprised her, for she assumed that he would yell out his demand at her. Lord Braden did touch her hand and she jumped at the contact.

Joanna looked at his face and, for a moment, she believed the words he spoke. She heard some promise, some enticement, buried deep within them and she wanted to take his hand. But, the stories and the terror grew inside of her until she could not bear it.

"Nay," she whispered. "Nay, I will not leave this place willingly to go with you."

She drew back her hand inside the cloak and wrapped her arms around her to await his response. Expecting an immediate and angry retort, she was amazed at the silence. And when she finally scraped enough courage together to dare a look at his face, she found him scrutinizing hers with a blank expression.

Lord Braden simply nodded at her and stepped back away. Turning, he walked swiftly to the door of the church and called to one of his men. After giving some quiet instructions, he faced her again.

"I do not understand your need to seek sanctuary here, Lady Joanna, but I have decided that I will not break the bond given by the priest. I will not interfere with your need to examine your conscience in this matter and make your peace with God and your confessor before coming with me." He smiled then, a wicked smile, and bowed to her and the lord and lady of Silloth. "Take whatever time you need, my lady."

Lord Braden waited at the door until his man returned. With her sack. He placed it on the bench and spoke. "My lord, if you will see to the lady's comforts as you offered, I would consider myself in your debt."

Stunned by his easy agreement, Joanna watched as Orrick and Margaret followed him out of the chapel. She could hear his words as he spoke of breaking their fast in the hall. Letting out her breath, she realized that she had lived through the worst moment of her life and that she was safe. When everyone was gone and the chapel returned to its quiet state and the sun shone outside the doorway, the truth of the situation struck her.

She had not gained a safe haven, she'd set up her own prison and Lord Braden, warlock of Wynwydd, held the key.

SIX

The next three days passed in a blur. Items for her comfort were delivered to the chapel, all by Lord Braden's order. He did not present himself during that time, but she spied him walking by the chapel a few times when she tried to enjoy the sun's warmth. Now, there was a wooden folding screen to give her a measure of privacy. A mattress overstuffed with feathers to use on top of the benches that formed her pallet. A chair and embroidering frame to keep her occupied through the day.

Her company increased as well in numbers and frequency. There were always several of Lady Margaret's women to share her meals and more in the evenings when the gossip and chatter turned to their favorite subject—their husbands.

The best things were the clean clothes and the bath. Two chemises, two gowns with matching tunics and new stockings. Soft leather slippers and even some veils to cover her unruly hair. Each time a servant arrived, it was all with the compliments of the lord of Wynwydd.

The bath was one she would never forget. The weeks

of being in the same clothes, sleeping on pallets on the floor and not washing off the dirt that offered her some disguise were horrible. Then, the bumps and bruises she'd gained on the journey and while here still hurt. And the backs of her thighs still stung and pulled when she moved. The evening of the day he said he'd not interfere, that first bath arrived.

One appeared each evening now and as she slid into the steaming water it was both pleasure and pain. However, Joanna would not have given it up for anything. Lady Margaret's own maid helped her through it. Her hair was washed and rinsed twice in a separate bucket and she soaked until the water cooled before getting out. Her body, now cleaned and soothed from its injuries, wanted only sleep.

Wearing a new chemise and covered with thick, warm blankets, Joanna could feel the pull of sleep on her. Even the thought that she was not alone could not keep her from it. In the shadows she noticed Lord Braden's cloak still hanging on a peg by the door. Then, the dream began and she was lost in it.

She traveled on a horse, down a road in a dark forest. The trees were so thick that no light broke through to show her the way ahead. Someone was behind her and she knew she must escape. The sounds of a horse and demonic laughter made her urge her mount to greater speeds. Then, the forest ended and she was trapped before a huge black castle. The walls grew as she watched and her pursuer stopped before her, blocking the way.

Joanna climbed down from the horse and tried to run around the other rider. He controlled the massive destrier without effort and her attempts were stopped. When he flew off the horse toward her, she backed against the wall and covered her face.

There was no way out.

Then the voices began, first whispers she could not hear and then accusations made louder and louder until they wailed like the wind around her.

"His father was mad."

"He killed his mother."

"The devil's own."

"Evil."

"Madness."

"He will not let you live knowing his secrets."

"You will die giving him a son or for not giving him one."

She turned and turned, looking for the source of the voices, but no one was there. Only him. In the shadows now where his face did not show. His cloak flowed around him like the clouds in a storm—dark, swirling, uncontrolled.

Then he stepped closer to her.

The scream caught in her throat as she saw his gleaming eyes and evil intent. Forced back as far as she could, her voice finally escaped and she let out a long, keening scream. On and on, with no one answering her plea for help.

Strong hands held her and shook her from the dream. When she forced her eyes open, the object of her nightmare sat next to her. She pushed him away, forced her way out of his grasp and slid back until she hit the cold stone wall. Even the protesting of her legs and bottom did not stop her from putting as much distance between them as she could.

"Joanna? Are you well?" he asked as he leaned over her. "You were screaming."

Images from the dream flooded her thoughts again and she saw the menacing look in his eyes. Blinking over and over, she watched as his face took shape. His eyes were filled with concern, not evil. His face no longer looked demonic, but just like a man. She tried to speak, tried to breathe, but her chest would not take any air in. Gasping, she tore at the blankets.

"Here now. Your thrashing has tied you up in these," he said as he grabbed the blankets and pulled them free. "Come away from the wall and sit on the edge." He took her hands to help her move forward and she dangled her legs over the side of the benches. Then, with one hand on her back and one on the top of her chest, he straightened her up. "Breathe now. Force my hands apart with your breaths."

The heat from his hands spread and soon Joanna was able to expand her chest and take in air. He quietly urged her on as she struggled with each inhalation and exhalation. After a few minutes, he released her and stepped away.

"Were you dreaming of me?" he asked from across the chamber. His voice was soft again, but his expression was heated. 'Twas as though he could look through her with his intense eyes. Then she realized that the light from the candles and the burning brazier exposed her in just her shift.

"Aye," she answered. Fearing to say more, she looked away from him and pulled one of the blankets around her shoulders.

"The fear is back in your gaze, my lady. I had hoped it was gone."

"Fear, my lord?"

"Aye, fear. I could see it there in every move you made and hear it in every word you spoke to me until just yesterday. I had hoped that it was gone."

Joanna did not answer him. The dream had simply reinforced all the terrible things she knew about him. 'Twould take more than a gift or two or a show of kindness to rid her of her fears about him.

"Will you answer me truthfully if I ask you some questions?" She decided it was time to face some of it.

"About my reputation?" He sounded tired, his voice flat now.

"Aye, my lord." She clenched her hands together and waited. Even if he said Aye, how would she know if it was the truth?

"Go ahead, lady, give me your questions." He walked to the wall nearest her little alcove and leaned against it, crossing his arms over his chest. Lord Braden closed his eyes for a moment and then looked over at her. "Well?"

"Did you father truly go mad?" This one was known across the land, so it was more for her use in gauging his replies.

"Aye, lady. My father was overcome by madness before my birth and died when I was a small boy." He shifted against the wall. "Next?"

"Did your grandfather throw himself and your grandmother off the tower of your castle to their deaths?"

He lifted his hand now and placed the heel of his palm against his forehead before answering. Lord Braden stood like that for several minutes before saying a word.

"'Tis true but not in the way you described, lady. My grandmother died giving birth to my father and my grandfather carried her to the tower and killed himself."

Part of her wanted to comfort him. To live with such a history, to have to live with such sadness. But, the next question was the one she feared the most for its subject was close to her own story but for the ending…at least so far. She hesitated to ask, but he nodded to her.

"I have been told that your previous betrothed begged her father to gain her release and that he offered you gold to release her." She paused now, for the rest was worse than that. Taking a breath, she blurted it out, "And when you refused to release her, she took her own life."

Joanna expected him to give some explanation to the accusation, but his reaction frightened her even more. He stood to his full height and turned his intensity to her. She shuddered at his approach and found herself held up against the wall by his harsh grasp.

"Damn them for speaking of it!" he growled at her. He shook her once and leaned in closer. "And damn you for listening!"

With another shake, he released her and she slid down until she touched the floor. She dared not move for his fury was a living thing. He swung his fist back, knocking down the wooden partition. Stomping on it until it broke, he kicked at the pieces and they scattered across the floor. Finished with that, he looked around as though searching for something else to destroy.

Joanna curled up into a ball and tried to protect her head and face, much as she'd done when her father did his worst. She heard his heavy footfalls and knew he stood before her. Saying a prayer in what she thought would be her last minute, she held her breath and hoped it would be over quickly. His panting was right next to her and she waited for the first blow to fall.

"Damn you," he whispered in a choking voice and then his steps moved away.

She dared a peek from behind her arms and watched him stumble from the chapel. The door stood no chance against his anger. It was pulled from its frame and, with a loud crash, fell to the floor. When his guard stepped forward, Lord Braden shoved him back and ran down the path.

In these past weeks, she'd never given in to the urge to cry. Now, the tears burned her eyes and rolled down her cheeks as any hopes she might have had of living through this crumbled. The anger inside of him was so great and so dangerous that she knew, with the wrong word or action, she could be its target.

Daylight crept in a few hours later and so did the servants. Without a word, the splintered partition was removed and a new one installed. A quiet unease reigned over the chapel, even through the Mass and later. All the gossip in the world could not lighten her mood. Now confronted with the truth of his character, Joanna knew she must escape the lord of Wynwydd.

But how?

He kept guards around the chapel and another near the front gates. Anything pertaining to her care was asked of him first. His scrutiny missed nothing.

For two days it rained and the weather made Joanna long for a walk outside this stone prison. Left on her own, most of her time over these past few years had been spent at the one remaining family estate in the woodlands of eastern England. With no one to tell her otherwise, she'd walk for miles, enjoying the sound of the birds and wildlife around her. Her own gardens were fruitful with herbs and plants and flowering bushes.

She would never see those gardens again. Never choose seedlings again. Never harvest the bounty of herbs her garden produced. The winds outside whipped around the buildings and wailed down the pathways of the yard. The mournful sounds matched her feelings. Now, she could only pace the forty steps front to back and twenty paces side to side that this church offered.

And walk them she did. She tried to exhaust herself so that she could sleep, but the dreams and worries kept rest from her. The leaky roof of the church did not help, for the rain dripped in several places with such force and regularity that it almost sounded like music to a song. A discordant song, though.

The thunderstorms woke her in the night and the heavy rain kept most away from her side. A servant would scurry in with her meal and then race through the raindrops back to the keep. Then on the third day of rain, things changed. Instead of just a meal, the servants brought out a table in pieces and assembled it in one corner. More arrived with linens and platters and goblets and pitchers of wine and ale and then all manner of foods. 'Twas much more than one or even two could eat.

Lord Orrick led the way, followed by Lady Margaret and then Lord Braden. Her betrothed appeared uncomfortable as he approached her. Joanna tried not to back away or shake as he took her hand and lifted it to his lips. Not usually the one for reticence, he would not meet her gaze as Lord Orrick began.

"My ladywife thought it might be worthwhile for the four of us to dine together. As the caretakers, or future caretakers, of a large number of souls and many acres of land and crops, there may be topics of mutual interest to us all."

The servants had finished their work and a square table, surrounded by four chairs and covered with linen cloths and platters of mouthwatering food, awaited them. Lord Orrick took her hand and led her to one of the chairs and she watched over her shoulder while Lord Braden did the same. Lady Margaret nodded to the servants and the meal proceeded.

Joanna ate silently as the two men exchanged ideas about the practice of crop rotation and the weather patterns of the past two growing seasons. When Lady Margaret brought up her own garden on the other side of the keep, Joanna joined in the talk.

"I would like your opinion on the layout of my newest herb garden, Joanna. I think it is the best place for it, but you can tell me what you think when you see it."

Silence spread as they each realized that Joanna would not see it as long as she stayed here.

"Actually, my lady, I have seen it. I delivered a cartful of manure to it the first week I worked in your stables." She felt their scrutiny and smiled. "'Twas my job then."

Orrick laughed at the situation and they all joined in. "And what think you of the layout? Is it like your own?"

"Nay, Lord Orrick," she began before he stopped her.

"As I explained to Braden, one of my eccentricities is my permission to use given names and not stand on 'lord this' or 'lady that.' If you have no objections?"

Such freedom existed here. The lord moved and lived among his people, his wife was forthright and outspoken, and all seemed right with it. Joanna's weeks at court had been exhausting for her as she tried to remember the correct titles and order of precedence that one lord had over another. With little else but the pomp to cling to, her parents would never have allowed this familiarity among their servants and serfs.

"None, my none, Orrick." He smiled at her with such kindness that she wanted to cry once more. Joanna swallowed the tears and answered the questions about the gardens. "My own is evenly split between cooking and healing herbs. But with your other estates pooling their resources, you may not need to do that here."

"And Wenda's adds to ours, as well," Margaret explained.

"As Gwanwyn will do at Wynwydd," Braden said. "She is known in both Wales and England for her healing abilities."

He still would not look at her as he spoke. The practice continued as the meal progressed and they talked on a range of topics including the king's recent second marriage, the possibility of being called to fight for their liege lord and the past glories of the Plantagenet kings.

Finally they finished the meal and Orrick offered to show her an intriguing family secret about the altar's design. She walked at his side to the front of the church as he explained the intricate pattern carved into the main stone of the altar.

"He feared that he had ruined any chance with you," Orrick whispered. "He asked for our assistance in taking this first step."

"Braden is afraid?" she asked, shaking her head. "He is angry and frightening and stubborn and—"

"Afraid, Joanna. This marriage to you means more to him than simply a wife and possible heirs. Whatever has happened to his family in the past has scarred him. His anger hides much of the real person inside him." Orrick outlined the carvings of his, his wife's and his children's names. "Something deep drives him and all he will tell me is that you are the one he must wed. And it must be accomplished soon."

"Do you know of his family, Orrick? Did he tell you of them?"

Orrick shook his head. "Nay, he would not. He would only say that there is more to know."

Joanna thought on his words. What did he hide? Could she bear it? Would she live through it?

"You were still ill when you came here. I know that now. I think your illness made you believe things that you otherwise would not have. I think it was the fever that made you run away. If you had been thinking clearly, none of this, or most of this, would not have happened." Orrick took her hand and clasped it in his. "He is not a warlock, Joanna. I think you know that somewhere inside of you, but the fear built by that fever's distortions is keeping its hold on you."

"But, is he evil, Orrick? Are the stories true?"

He was correct—a part of her recognized that the magical powers attributed to Braden were fabrications of scared minds.

"All men are both good and evil, Joanna. And so much of the balance depends on those around him."

"Orrick?" Margaret called out to him. "I wish to retire."

"Joanna, these old eyes see a man molded by his family's misfortunes, surrounded by rumors and tales, who is searching for a way for his name and family to survive. He has pinned his hopes on you. Are you strong enough to be the woman he needs?"

Orrick held out his arm and Joanna placed her hand on top of his. "Think on my words, Joanna."

Joanna watched as Orrick and Margaret took their leave and then she stood aside as the servants efficiently removed all traces of the meal from the chapel. It was soon only the two of them.

Braden was not certain that the meal had been an effective first step, but she was not backing away from him. A good sign, surely. Now, the difficult part. He cleared his throat and coughed a few times.

"May I stay a while longer, Joanna?"

She walked to one of the remaining chairs and sat down. "If you wish, my lord."

"Please. Can we not follow the example of our host and use our given names?" At her nod, he sat facing her in the other chair. "I would like to apologize for hurting you. I truly did not mean to, not the other night or when I found you in the stables. And yet, I know that I have."

Her hand strayed to her neck and the bruises that were now a mix of blues, greens and purples. In truth, he wanted to soothe those and all the others she must carry from the rough journey she made. Margaret reported that she was quite battered and only now was moving without pain.

"And I would ask your pardon for terrifying you with such behavior as you saw here. Sometimes… sometimes…"

He searched for a way to tell her that she was not the cause. The catalyst mayhap, but not the cause. He had worn himself out in the yard these past days trying to drain the rage from him. One after another of Orrick's knights had challenged him and he had exhausted his strength there so that he would have none with her.

"My father always told me that I had the most annoying way of angering him, too. His reaction was much the same as yours."

Her focus drifted into the shadows with her matter-of-fact words, but he heard more in them than she probably realized she was saying. Her hands opened and closed as he watched, like fists being formed. Whose fists?

"I will not strike you, Joanna. I have never struck a woman in my life and will not begin now."

She looked at him now and he saw her chin tilt out just a bit. "Why do you want me, Braden? Why did you choose me?"

He smiled at her. Just as she might be beginning to believe he was only a man, and a flawed one at that, his words would make him sound mad.

"'Tis apparent that some kind of affliction has beset the last generations of my family. I sought relief from it and finally a wise-woman in my village told me to seek out a woman 'of black' and to marry her in the fullness of spring. She said that my son—" Braden stared at her as he continued "—our son would end this affliction."

He waited for her reaction. Only her hands trembled. Then she searched his face and must have read the seriousness of his intentions there.

"You want me because of my name?"

"Your name was the first thing that gained my attention. Joanna of Blackburn. Then when you were pointed out to me, your black hair seemed a confirmation of it."

Her hand went to her hair, or what was left of it. "And I cut it off to elude you. Will it nullify the prophesy if I cut it?"

She gifted him with a smile that lit up her face the way it had been when she stood in the sun at the doorway. Her laughter, full and generous, touched his soul and he felt something other than despair for the first time in such a long time.

"I know this sounds foolish, Joanna, but I've lived with the prospect of going mad since my father did. And back through five generations, the lords of Wynwydd have been cur—afflicted with this tendency. The only hope in all of my searching is Gwanwyn's words."

He stood and approached her chair. Going down onto one knee at her side, Braden took her hand in his. "Even if none of this is true, even if it is only cruel coincidence that afflicts my family, I still need a bride and find that I want you in spite of our less-than-fortuitous beginning."

"Your mother died birthing you?" she asked in a soft voice.

He would not lie now. "Aye."

"And no male relatives survive? You are the only one left?"

"Aye." He would not turn away.

"You have no powers?"

"Nay. I know the gossip, Joanna. The lords of Wynwydd are not evil wizards or mages. We do not lay curses on others. Indeed, 'twould appear that due to some long-ago wrong, we are the ones cursed. I confess though, to encouraging some of the gossip, for it gave us some measure of privacy against the greedy or curious when we were feared."

"I have one more question, but I hesitate to ask it of you."

"Is it about Cecily? The woman I was betrothed to?" He knew this was her test of him, of his control, but he worried over his reaction. She nodded her head. "Ask your question."

She slid her hand from his and clasped her hands together in her lap. Well, 'twas better than holding them in front of her face as he'd last seen her do.

"Did you cause her death?"

Braden stood and walked to the door. He feared the results of failing her test, but did not have the strength of heart to speak of Cecily with her. Nor with anyone. He pulled the now-repaired door open and stepped outside. Turning and seeing the surprise on her face, he nodded to her.

"Aye, Joanna. Her death was at my hands and marked against my soul, but I cannot, will not, speak of it with you."

Closing the door, he walked back to his chambers and fell onto the bed. Defeat was pressing in on him. When he wanted to give her words that would have convinced her of the rightness of his course, he could not. When he wanted to explain his part in Cecily's horrifying end, he could not.

Sleep did not come easily that night. Even as the

storms outside dissipated, the ones in his heart and in his soul strengthened. There were but a few weeks left of spring and he knew that his chances of getting Joanna to leave the church had lessened with tonight's frankness.

If he believed in Gwanwyn's words, she was his one chance.

As seemed to be the pattern over the past week, the sun shone brightly on the morning after the three days of storms. He woke just as confused over his future as he'd felt when he'd finally drifted off to sleep. The warmer winds signaled that spring was gaining control over the days of winter. But his own life spun out of control.

Orrick's man Royce had invited Braden to train again this morn and he was on the way there now. His feet however took the long way to the yard, the one that passed the church.

As certain as he was that the days were growing longer, he was more certain that he would find her there, stretching as far as she could to feel the sun on her face. Braden turned onto the path and looked at the low stone building on his right. Joanna was exactly where he knew she would be. Although every part of her was legitimately in the church with her toes on the end of the stone doorstep, she somehow managed to balance herself without falling out.

Braden stopped and watched her for a moment. She wore a gown now, and the soft material of it flowed over her womanly curves, enhancing not hiding them from him. A scarf of some kind wrapped loosely around her shoulders hid most of the damage he'd done to her when he'd captured her in the stables.

She would be the perfect wife for him for all of the reasons that Orrick had mentioned and several others of his own. She was bold and there was a passion in her that he wanted to taste. She was intelligent. And, from the expression on her face as he had told of his mother's death and father's madness, she was compassionate. She knew when she was wrong and could accept her errors, and she fought valiantly when she thought she was right.

She was his.

Braden recognized the feeling that was becoming stronger within him for Joanna, but worried that the outcome would be the same as for the last woman he loved. He had driven Cecily from his side with words of hate, and she had met her death because of him. No matter that his intentions had been to save her from his fate. No matter that her father had agreed. No matter that he had loved her more than anyone in his life. Cecily was dead and he was still trying to cheat his fate.

He did not plan to love Joanna as he had Cecily, though. The death of another loved one would surely send him to the brink of the same madness that had claimed his father. Was that the cause, then? The loss of so many loved ones and family members and the failure to somehow make it stop. If he followed this foolhardy plan and it did not work, was that his fate, as well?

Braden walked up to the stone fence and stood by the gate. The sun warmed the morning air and all it touched. The breezes moved over the yard, and he watched as they lifted and teased her now-clipped hair. She laughed and the sound of it warmed him. Then she opened her eyes and saw him.

He held his breath and waited to see if she would turn and run inside as she had the last time. Or would she simply turn away with disdain over his admissions last evening?

"Good morning, my lord," she said quietly.

"I thought we had decided to use our given names, Joanna."

She leaned her head in the direction of the guard as though his presence was the cause. "Your people will surely think it unseemly, my lord."

Braden nodded to the guard and stepped closer, using care not to block the sun's rays from her. "My people would think that most of what I do is unseemly. But, while here in Orrick's domain, we can follow his example."

She nodded and stood quietly as he watched. Within minutes, the doorway would be in the shade and any warmth would be lost to her until the next morn. He'd noticed the dampness and chill inside the building last evening during the meal and now realized that it must be a terrible loss to someone who loved the out-of-doors as much as she did.

She must be very serious about her objections to him to willingly deprive herself of the spring breezes and blossoms and all the other signs of the earth's renewing. Joanna was not being frivolous in claiming sanctuary if it resulted in the loss of her favorite season and most likely her only pleasurable memories.

He held out his hand to her without much more thought on it. "Come, Joanna, step into the spring's fullness."

Joanna stepped back and shook her head. "I cannot."

So, her fears were not yet gone or managed. He must give her some sign, some way for her to know him better and to put those fears behind her.

"As I see it, the stones in this pathway touch those of the church's doorway so they are part of the chapel building and part of the place where you claim sanctuary. You would be safe from interference while on those stones."

He watched the hesitation in her eyes war with the desire to take that step, not only out into the spring but also with him. Braden moved closer and reached for her.

"I give my word that I consider the path to be part of the church."

Joanna looked from his face to his hand to the flat stones at their feet and back to his face. He held his breath as he waited to see if she would take this step in trust.

SEVEN

Joanna stared at Braden with his hand outstretched to her and thought he had never looked more like an enchanter than at that moment. His long dark hair hung to his shoulders and threw shadows onto his chiseled features. His green eyes glimmered in the sun's light and his smile was pure temptation. His offer, though only for a step into the gorgeous spring morning, spoke of much, much more when she looked into those eyes.

He was asking for her trust.

Could she give it? Could she not?

Braden gave his word and she would love to escape from the dismal confines of the church and feel the sun and smell the flowers she could see from her perch on the doorstep. She wanted to see the green grass filling in around the yard and see how far the ivy crept on the walls of the church.

Joanna looked at his hand and grasped it for the chance it was. His fingers curled around hers and she stepped down onto the path, out of the church for the first time in over a sennight. Then, with another step, she was fully engulfed in the warmth of the sun and the breezes that moved through the yard.

"My lord," the guard said, approaching them. "You have her now! We can go."

Joanna felt Braden's grasp tighten as he shook his head and held out his other hand to stop the guard's approach. "Nay, Raymund, I gave the lady my word. Her sanctuary extends on these stones to yonder gate. Let her be."

Daring one step then another, Joanna walked down the path to the stone fence and its bounty of flowers. Irises, eglantine, even monkshood and wild roses, all displayed their blossoms and, as she moved closer, their scents. After watching them opening over this past week and not being able to enjoy them, Joanna breathed in deeply now.

When he dropped her hand, Joanna turned around and around trying to capture all the images of the newly alive season—flowers, the sound of birds in the trees outside the keep's walls, newly sprouted grass that filled in many empty spots in the yard's dirt and along the keep's walls and buildings.

'Twas spring in earnest in Silloth.

Her gardens in the south of England must be past full bloom. Who would look after them now?

"Why are you sad? I thought it would please you to be free of the church for a time?" he asked as he walked to where she stood.

"It does please me, greatly, Braden. I just thought of my own gardens and how there will be no one to tend them now."

"You will have new challenges as lady of Wynwydd, Joanna. I assure you that you will not find my lands wanting as a place to grow your plants and herbs."

They stood together at the fence and Joanna pointed out and named the various flowers and plants that grew there. Many passersby stopped and stared at her appearance outside the church. She knew they must think her turmoil over and her decision made, but she did still fear the punishments he would mete out for her disobediences and humiliations.

"You have that worried look again, Joanna. Tell me why." He offered his hand and she took it. He led her to a wooden bench inside the gate and they sat.

"I wish not to ruin this wonderful moment, Braden."

"If 'tis some worry that I can soothe, tell me." He lifted her hand to his lips and kissed the back of it, sending shivers through her. "I would clear up any misunderstandings between us as soon as possible."

She needed to discover if her beatings and mistreatments were at his order. If he had done so before, he would do so again, especially if he were in his home and answered to no one. Joanna moved a bit over from him so she could look at his face when she asked.

"Would you consider the beatings I have already

received to be sufficient punishment for my misdeeds or do you plan to order more?"

"Beatings?" he asked in a soft voice. "What do you mean?"

"My parents made certain that I knew they were carrying out your wishes with every blow and with every lash. I just wonder if you consider that enough or if you will seek more."

"Beatings?" he asked louder now. "My orders?" He stood and shouted now. "I ordered no such thing!"

"But I heard your words to my father. You demanded my consent at any cost."

His face was red with anger and he clenched his teeth as he took a few steps away and returned. He towered over her and she began to back away when she realized that any steps away from him would take her off the stone path. Joanna gathered up her skirts and ran back inside the chapel. Once inside, she knew there was nowhere to run from him.

"Tell me of these beatings," he whispered. She could tell he was trying to control his rage. "Tell me what was done in my name."

Joanna did not want to face him when she spoke of her shame, so she looked away instead. "My father has a servant who he uses for just such things. This man can punish and leave little trace. When I would not agree to the marriage, they began by withholding my food and then he was sent to me."

She tried to keep the images from her thoughts, but she could not. Her father had watched as she was pummeled with fists and open hands. She'd managed to pick herself up the first few times she'd fallen, but the rest was a blur.

"When did this happen?" He was closer now, but off to one side.

"Right after I spoke in front of the king. My father threatened me with everything he could, including your reputation. He said only my swift compliance would save my life and my soul."

"And you would not. What was it that frightened you the most and caused your refusal?"

"The story about your ability to curse souls. And the one about the fate of your betrothed." She dared a glance at him now. "I did not want to die, Braden. I do not, but somehow any fate that ended with me as your wife seemed to involve my death."

He would not meet her eyes. How much was false and how much was truth?

"A few nights later, just after you demanded that I be brought to your lands, my father began in earnest to force my compliance. First with the cane and then with the lash. I remember not ever giving my consent, but I admit to those next days and nights blurring together."

She shivered as the memories of the sting and then burning of the cane's touch came once more. She thought she had held her tongue during that. Not until the lash tore her skin and she was weak from the loss of blood did she think she uttered the words of her surrender. Then the fear for her immortal soul rather than her life took over and she formed the ill-advised plan to run to her sister's home for refuge.

"I think Orrick correct when he said that the fever drove me here. I only know that my thoughts turned to running from you and whatever else you had planned. If I could not save my life, I would save my soul from your evil purposes."

The expression on his face was one she'd not seen before. Horror filled his face. His mouth and eyes strained with it.

"I hurt you when I touched your back that night?"

Remembering the kiss and the caresses that had touched her bottom and back, she nodded. "Wenda said they will not stop hurting until they are completely healed."

"I would look on them," he said, approaching her now.

"No!" she said, retreating. "There is no need."

Never would she have thought that would be his reaction. But her objections did nothing to slow him. He reached for her and pulled her behind the screen to the pallet. Sitting down, he grasped her arms and placed her over his lap facedown.

"Please, my lord," she argued, trying to hold her skirts in place. "Do not do this."

"I do not wish to hurt you more, Joanna. If you lie

quietly, this will be over quickly. Struggle and it will take longer, but I mean to look on the results of the words I spoke in anger."

He was so much stronger that fighting him was useless, and she acquiesced in this. Trying not to imagine what he would see, she felt the heat of embarrassment growing in her face as he lifted her tunic and gown to her waist. Only her shift hid the rest of her from his view. With a soft touch, he slid his hand along her thighs, over her bottom to her waist taking the layer of linen with it.

His indrawn breath told her more than words would. She could not see what they looked like, but she was sure that the scars would be ugly even when healed. As a warrior he must have seen the like before. And, if she did become his wife, any physical relations they had would be in the dark so he would never look on them again.

He placed his hand, large and warm, on the small of her back and she could hear only the faintest whisper under his breath. Then, he replaced her clothing and helped her to stand next to him. When she finally tamped down the terrible embarrassment she felt at this exposure and could finally meet his gaze, she was unprepared for the pain she saw there.

"I—" he began. "I—"

His words came out in an indistinguishable stutter until he stopped and shook his head. Then without another word, he walked past her and out of the chapel.

Joanna raced to the door but dared no farther. He disappeared from her view a moment later.

Braden took the sword from one of his men and climbed over the fence into the training yard. Although more dangerous than practicing with wooden ones or with quarterstaffs, both he and Royce were experienced enough to do it without killing each other. Since this was not warfare and the day was getting hotter, they stripped down to their breeches and, at the call of the weapon master, they began.

Braden lost himself in the steps of the fight that came without thought after so many years. Royce was more than competent, and Braden had the feeling that he had seen the man fight before. With the practiced moves of a champion, his opponent blocked Braden's usually successful thrusts and parries.

Soon, those gathered to watch began betting on the outcome of the fight and he felt the intensity of the weapons play rise. 'Twas at the worst possible time, as he struggled to keep ahead of Royce, that his thoughts turned back to Joanna.

He was no stranger to cruelty and had seen any number of examples of it across England, but none had turned his stomach so thoroughly as the marks and scars on her body. No wonder she flinched at his touch and feared his actions. If she thought him the cause—and she did—he had no chance of her coming willingly to his side. Inviting certain death was not only madness, it was stupidity, and Joanna suffered from neither.

Even if he had calmed her fears over the rumors of supernatural powers, she would be a fool to put herself in the hands of a man who would have the power of life and death and the infliction of such punishments over her. And she was not a fool.

The shouts brought him back to the fight and he felt the tip of the blade as it sliced the skin on his chest. Blood trickled down his stomach, but it was a mere scratch. He motioned to Royce to continue and he went on the attack. He forced Royce backward from his onslaught and laughed as he finally took control. He managed to nick Royce's arm and now his opponent's blood mixed with his in the dirt of the yard.

Had hers left a trail across England? Was that the source of her illness and fever? Every mark on her spoke of deep, bleeding wounds, wounds that would have been painful and would have drained her strength and life as she ran away.

From him.

From being his wife.

From tying her fate to the lords of Wynwydd.

He stumbled and his sword barely deflected Royce's swing. Regaining his balance, sweat dripped into his eyes and he swiped at it with his hand. Too late he spied Royce approaching from his side and, as he tried to move out of the reach of his sword, he felt it cut into his side and down onto his thigh. Startled at the pain, Braden fell back, never seeing the rock tucked into the dirt of the yard.

Oblivion reached up and claimed him.

The voices reached into the tranquility of the chapel and gained her attention. She walked to the door and crouched down to see the source of it. A crowd, mostly men, from the look and sound of it, was running to the keep from the yards where Orrick trained his men. She recognized a few of Braden's men in the lead as they came closer. They did not pause, but she could see that they carried someone on a plank of wood between them.

Braden.

All she could see was his dark hair and his blood-covered body as they ran past her. Then, she could see nothing of them. Loud voices called out orders. Her guard walked to the end of the path and watched as they carried his lord.

"Raymund, you must go and discover what has happened to your lord!" she called to him. "Go now!"

He hesitated, torn between his duty to his lord and his duty to stay there, but after a few moments, he ran off to the keep.

Was Braden dead? How had it happened? Joanna

knew he'd been training with Orrick's men, but they were not supposed to be real battles. She shivered as she remembered the moment that the crowd had moved and she saw the blood pouring from his head. Would he die?

Turning around, she realized that no one was in the yard. No one between the chapel and the keep. And from the silence that covered the area, no one between the chapel and the gates.

Her stomach clenched. Joanna knew that this was the best time to get away. She was healed and well rested and stood her best chance of completing her journey north. She noticed the sack of clothing she'd pushed under her pallet.

She could escape.

Grabbing the sack and the scraps of bread and cheese from her morning meal, she stepped outside and peered around the yard. Convinced that the way was clear, she ran from the chapel, through the gate and toward the walls of the keep. Still not seeing anyone paying attention to her, she crept nearer the open gates that led to the village and freedom.

A few more paces was all that stood between her and escape from Braden. Then, her chest tightened and she realized that she no longer feared him as she had before. Was he still alive in the keep? She did not want him to die.

The urge to run dissolved.

She wanted to have the chance to talk with him, to

come to some agreement with him about his plans and her place in them. She needed to hear the truth about his family from him. They might have a future together once he explained his past.

She might give up her claim to sanctuary if she understood.

Joanna turned now and ran to the keep, up the stairs that led to the great hall. Following the clamor, she found what she was looking for. Lady Margaret and Wenda were at his side, washing the blood and repairing some damage. Most stood back a bit watching the women work, so she had no difficulty reaching his side.

"How can I help, my lady?" she asked.

"Joanna, what are you doing here?" the lady asked. Pointing something out to Wenda, Margaret met her gaze. "You should not be here."

"I had to find out if Braden lived. What happened?"

"He took a deep slash in his side," Wenda said as she probed the wounds. "At least two ribs are broken and this will take cauterizing to stop the bleeding."

"Why is he not awake?"

"He hit his head on a rock as he fell, my lady," the knight called Royce said.

"Will he die?"

"If he wakes soon, I think he will recover," Wenda said. "He is strong, with a reason to heal."

Joanna knew the old woman spoke of her.

Then, with a loud groan, Braden opened his eyes. At first his focus moved from person to person and then it settled on her. She smiled at him, pleased that he was not seriously hurt.

"Joanna," he whispered.

He held out his hand to her and she took it. Moving closer so she could hear his words over the work of those who cared for him, she leaned down. "How do you fare?"

"You are mine."

He'd said that several times before, but there was a strangeness to it now. His grasp tightened. Joanna tried to retreat and found his hold was like an iron cage on her hand. She looked at him and noticed that his eyes were clear, as was his intent. His words merely confirmed it.

"Miles. Take her until I can see to her. In my chambers, tied if need be to keep her here."

"Braden," she whispered, shaking her head in disbelief. "No. I have sanctuary."

"Once you stepped out of the church, you lost that claim, Joanna."

Sick to her stomach, she looked around at those closest and saw the truth of his words. In coming to him, she'd surrendered herself, and before she had any assurances. She'd trusted him earlier but 'twas evident now that it was simply a ploy to lull her to his side.

Joanna did not struggle or fight back as Braden's men surrounded her and took her from the hall. Up the stairs they went, to the chambers assigned to Braden during his stay here. Miles held her wrist firmly all the way and entered the room with her.

"Must I restrain you here, my lady?"

She ignored his question and walked to the window in the room. Lifting the leather flap, she peered out. The chapel sat squarely in view below, taunting her for her stupidity.

"My lady?" Miles repeated, waiting for her compliance.

She would not say the words he wanted. She looked at him and then sought the only chair in the room. Leaning her head back, she closed her eyes.

The guard stepped out of the room and gave orders to the others. Just as the door closed, she heard the words that broke her heart.

"My lord said he would get her out of that church however he could. I will not doubt him again."

The mocking laughter of his men tore into her and Joanna put her face in her hands and cried for all that she'd lost.

He'd not expected her to surrender gracefully after all she'd risked in her attempt to escape him. Indeed, the warrior in him respected the efforts it had taken her to do what she had done. But the change in her was completely unforeseen.

Other than the two broken ribs, Braden's injuries were more flesh wounds and he'd spent two days healing before leaving for his home. In those two days and in the two days that they'd been on the road, she'd spoken not a word to him. The worst thing was that she was not sulking. She did not cast him angry looks. She did not whisper under her breath.

She was not the same.

When he asked her questions about the trees and plants around them, she did not respond. When he tried to tell her of his home, she said nothing. When he tried to explain that he could not have ignored the opportunity in the hall that morning, she looked through him. In place of the woman who had angered and intrigued and interested him was an empty shell of a person.

The fight was gone from her. The spirit was gone. The passion was gone. He had regained the woman and would have a wife but, as Orrick warned, he would not have a partner.

Braden tried to convince himself that she knew more about him now and would not fear him as she had at first. He had been as patient as he could in giving her time to learn about the man he truly was and he tried to persuade himself that she would come around once they settled at Wynwydd. The arguments and his answers rang hollow even to his ears.

He had betrayed her trust. She had come to him when she could have run and he had handed her over to his men. After three days on the road south, he realized what he must do.

EIGHT

Braden assisted Joanna out of the tent and to a place where she could take care of her personal needs. They broke their fast with the plain fare of travelers—bread, cheese, and ale. As his men readied their horses according to his orders, Braden took her aside to explain the change in plans.

"I have asked four of my men to escort you to your sister's home in Scotland. Miles will make any arrangements necessary along the way."

She looked at him for the first time in many days.

"I will send word to your father that I found your dead body and that our agreement is at an end."

The words tore him apart, but he knew it was the only way. In searching his thoughts and his intentions, he finally realized that the true curse of his family was in believing that anyone was expendable in their quest for release from their situation. He'd taken her against her desire and was willing to sacrifice her life and future to protect his own.

"My lord?" Her eyes searched his face as she tried to understand.

"My family has been cursed somehow for the last five generations. No male lives to see his heir or is sane enough to recognize him. Our women, our wives, seem not to be immune either. Many die in childbirth. 'Twould appear that I am the last of the lords of Wynwydd."

He turned and peered off into the forest around them. Spring's fullness had reached northern England and taunted him for his failure.

"Each generation has sought answers and relief from what seemed to be happening, but we have failed. When I realized the fruitlessness, 'twas too late." He pressed the heel of his palm against his forehead.

"I loved Cecily with all my heart and soul and wanted nothing so much as to have her as my wife," he began. He must explain this to her.

"Then my last uncle died and my cousin's wife died giving birth to a son. I realized that marrying her would simply make her suffer from the curse as the rest of us. Death and madness were all that lay before us."

He swallowed and tried to continue. Cecily's face as he ended their betrothal swam before him.

"She would not agree to end it, so I paid her father to do so. She ranted, raved and begged me not to end it so, but it was the only way I had to protect her. When the dispensation was granted and a new match arranged for her, she came to Wynwydd and we argued. Thinking it would be easier for her to bear if she hated me, I said terrible things to her."

The sounds of that night, the words of anger, and the look on her face would haunt him until the end of his days. Even worse, finding her broken body after her horse had thrown her and knowing she had died hating him.

"Her horse threw her as she rode out of Wynwydd and she died that night."

He took Joanna's hand and led her to her horse. "I will not watch another woman I love die because of my family. I will not take a wife when I know now that I want a partner, like Orrick of Silloth has."

Braden lifted her up onto the horse's back and handed her the reins. "I release you from our betrothal, Joanna. Go now and I hope you find some measure of happiness in your life and a husband who will not betray your trust as I did."

If he thought or hoped that she might say something, he was disappointed. As Miles led the way north out of their camp, she simply stared at him as they rode away.

As he'd told her, he had learned so much from Orrick and Margaret of Silloth. And from all of their people. But, all that he had learned about himself and about what he truly wanted was for naught.

Joanna watched the backs of two of Braden's men as they rode back the way they'd come from Silloth. Miles told her they would travel to Carlisle and then on to Scotland. With so many traveling to and from that city, their appearance would not gain the attention of anyone. No need for a disguise this time.

Try as she might, she was not able to wipe the sight and sound of Braden from her memory or from her heart. When he had ordered her held, she was prepared to hate him. She wanted to come to him after her questions were answered and after she knew what to expect from him.

Now, she had all the answers but no Braden.

No wonder he was angry at fate for dealing such a horrible burden to his family. He watched as everyone he cared for perished in unspeakable ways. And not by his hand as the gossips reported.

What would be her fate as his wife? Would he go mad as his father had? Would she die in childbirth, trying to give him a son? Or was she the one chance to change the fate of his family as Gwanwyn had foretold?

As she thought on his words, she remembered the reason he'd given in sending her away and finally understood that, if he could send her away to protect her, he was the man she wanted to marry. The kind of man she would be safe with. The kind of man who would be her husband and her partner in the challenges that life had to offer.

The kind of man she could love.

"Miles!"

She would always remember the look on his face as she and his men caught up with him on the road.

Shock.

Confusion.

Love.

And such hope that she cried as she saw it in his eyes. Joanna slid down from her horse and rushed into his arms. He caught her and held her as though he'd never let her go. Then, the stupid man began to try to talk her out of her decision.

"I may go mad."

"As might I, Braden, if you force me away."

He kissed her for that comment, his hands ruffling her hair and his tongue tasting her mouth.

"You might die in childbirth," he whispered, his voice filled with the fear of losing her.

"Aye, I may. All women might. But, with Gwanwyn's help, it should work out."

Braden held her closely and nuzzled her head with his chin.

"'Twas only after you let me go that I knew you were not the man I believed you to be. Or should I say you are the man I hoped you would be."

"Are you certain about this, Joanna? I could not bear it if you ran from me again."

"As certain as any woman can be, Braden. Unless there is something you have not shared with me that I need to know?"

He leaned back and looked into her eyes and she saw amusement within his. "Only a few surprises that I would not want to spoil for you, love."

EPILOGUE

The first of the surprises was Wynwydd itself.

Somehow, she'd expected dark brooding forests and shadowed landscapes to match the reputation of the lords of Wynwydd. As they crossed the last stream and entered his lands, Joanna was astonished to find green, rolling hills, lush forests, clear blue lakes and farmlands that looked as plentiful as any she'd seen.

Any hint that his people lived in fear of him vanished as they entered the village outside his walled manor house. He called out her name to them and they cheered her arrival. His people crowded around as they said their vows twice—once at the doors of the church and once under a bower of the most beautiful blossoms and vines she'd ever seen.

The second surprise was Gwanwyn.

For some reason, she had the image of an older woman, one of an age such as Lady Margaret or Wenda, in mind whenever Braden mentioned the wise-woman of his village. Instead, Gwanwyn was a well-endowed young woman of not more than a score of years with a lithesome figure, bright blue eyes and shimmering locks of blond hair, hair that would have rivaled her own, before she cut it off.

Joanna's attempts to tamp down the jealous feelings when she saw this woman talking in a familiar manner with Braden did not go unnoticed. Indeed, she was so surprised by Gwanwyn's true appearance that he had to reach over and close her mouth when he introduced them.

But the biggest surprise happened after their wedding.

After Braden claimed her and made her his own, she had drifted off to sleep. Sometime later, he roused her from her sleep and carried her outside. Wrapped in only a cloak, she huddled in his arms as the guards opened the gate and he walked back to the same bower where they had spoken their vows earlier.

"Braden, why are we here?" she asked in a whisper as he placed her back on her feet. "Someone could hear us or see us."

"'Tis the part of Gwanwyn's words that I did not tell you about, Joanna. A surprise. Fear not, love, no one will approach this place until after dawn."

He slipped his hands inside the cloak and touched her breasts. The chill of the air and the heat of his hands made for an enticing feeling and she leaned into him. Knowing now what was to come, Joanna leaned her head back and accepted his kiss. His tongue swirled around hers and he traced circles around the tightened buds of her nipples with his thumbs. Arching into his hands, she kissed him back, sucking on his tongue and lifting his tunic to reach inside.

Before she could stop him, he tore off his tunic and untied the laces of her cloak, dropping it on the ground behind her. Gooseflesh rose on her skin and she started to pull away. Instead, Braden rubbed his hands down her back, onto her bottom and pulled her closer to him so that his heated skin touched hers. And warmed her.

The pulsing heat spread through her as he touched and teased her body. Still new at this part of it, Joanna wrapped her hands around his neck and held on tightly as he took her once more on this journey of love. She felt his hardness against her belly and knew that he would claim her soon.

Braden knelt before her and kissed all the way down from her breasts to her stomach and then even onto the curls that shielded that most private part of her. When he spread her legs and tried to put his mouth there, she startled.

"Braden?"

"Too soon then, love? We can try that in our bed. For now…" he said, his words trailing off into a whispered promise.

He sat back on his heels and guided her to straddle his legs, bringing the place that now throbbed onto his hardness. When she hesitated, he teased the aching folds between her thighs with his hands and eased her down. As he filled her, her head fell back and Joanna moaned out the wonderful feelings within her. Then, shifting once more, he laid her on her back and thrust as deeply as he could.

Surrounded by the soft green grass, the scent of nearby honeysuckles and the sounds of the approaching dawn, she felt everything within her tighten as she met his thrusts with her own. Her toes curled and she drew her legs up so that he could enter more deeply into her body. Aching, she welcomed his hardness against the core of her. Moving together and apart, together and apart, she could feel the tension within her growing and growing until, with a last thrust, he spilled his seed inside of her.

Her own release welled up from the core of her, through her heart and soul, and out until her cries mingled with his. Their essences spilled out on the grass, now covered with the morning dew.

They stayed joined, until they could breathe again and then he eased from her. Although her body had begun to notice the morning's chill air, she was still too caught up in the throes of their joining to complain.

"Did you feel it?" he asked, turning on his side and gazing on her. He slid his hand down and rested it on her belly.

"I felt much." She smiled at him and reached out to entwine her fingers with his.

"Gwanwyn said the curse would be lifted if we joined in such a manner."

Shaking her head, she wondered if she should be fearful of the power of Gwanwyn over her husband. Then, realizing what the wise-woman's words had done, she decided not.

"And do you believe it, Braden? Is it gone?"

"I hope so, love. I hope so."

They were not completely alone.

'Twas Gwanwyn's practice to gather certain herbs at dawn when they were just opening and most potent. She skirted the bower not wanting to intrude, but the sound of a woman's keening release and a man's deep groan of satisfaction could be heard throughout the valley.

The lord of Wynwydd had found his life mate and brought her back to his home.

Her words, her prophecies as Lord Braden called them, were not really a magic spell or enchantment. They were the simple words of someone who recognized the danger of hopelessness. For once a man lost hope, he lost all and could hold nothing.

Her own family had lived on this land and served the lords of Wynwydd for generations as ill fortune met disaster and the family was nearly destroyed—first by untimely deaths and then by the growing gossip and rumors about them.

Lord Braden's father did not heed the words of her

mother, nor his grandfather before him. 'Twas only when Braden came to manhood and showed the spark of knowledge and the willingness to listen that she could fulfill her family's calling and help him lift the true curse that plagued them.

And it was only through a woman like Joanna that it could work. Only with Joanna's demand for him to change, and her love and support for him, could he learn to hope again.

And hope was the answer he sought.

Even as the light of dawn crept over the horizon, the laughter of the lord and lady spilled down the valley and across the meadows. Gwanwyn smiled and entered the forest assured that the curse was gone and, in nine months' time, the lord of Wynwydd would look upon his heir.

Please turn the page to enjoy an excerpt from

The King's Mistress

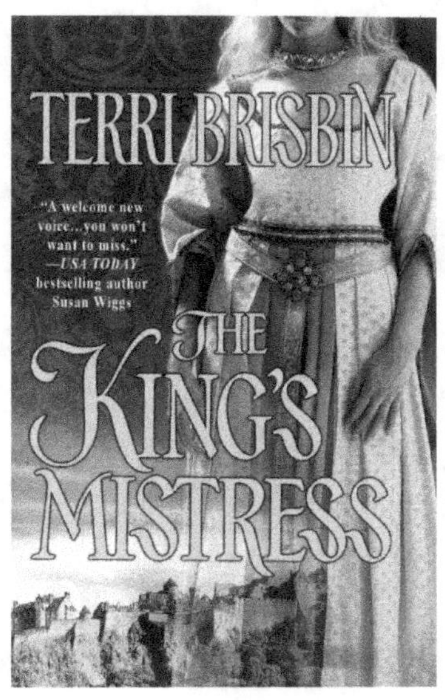

"My lady," he said as he acknowledged her obeisance and held out his hand. "Please rise now."

The softness of her fingers against his work-roughened hand sent fire through him. And when she finally raised her gaze to his, he knew he was lost.

Her hair did indeed reach nigh to the floor in spite of some decorations and jewels that were woven into the curls surrounding her face. His hands itched to touch it, feel it, even bring it to his face and inhale the fragrance of her that was carried by it. When she moved her head, her hair cascaded in flowing waves over her shoulders and arms and down her back. In an instant, his mind pictured her how she would be later in the night—in his bed, naked, with only her hair to shield her.

Shocked by his carnal reaction to simply meeting her, Orrick knew he must tame this beast within him or appear the barbarian she surely thought him to be. Stepping back and motioning to a bench, he allowed her to sit. A few steps across the chamber and he felt a bit more in control. Until she spoke.

"My lord Orrick, I am pleased to have this chance to meet you privately. My thanks for granting what must seem a strange request by a bride on her wedding day."

Soft and incredibly feminine, her voice carried within a hint of huskiness and once more his body betrayed him. That underlying tone would be evident as she cried out her pleasure in his bed. He saw her naked and writhing against him as he filled her with his seed and as their satisfaction poured forth from both of them in loud cries. He closed his eyes for a moment and then realized her power.

Orrick had come to this day aware of the gossip and the tales told about her ongoing liaisons with the king. He had armed himself with a healthy measure of suspicion so that he did not become anyone's fool in this. Believing that he did not make decisions with his cock, he had felt completely at ease with his ability to assess the lady and the situation and handle all of it.

Fool!

In but a few moments, her beauty, her blatant sexuality and her silent promises about what would be his ensorcelled him. With a curtsy and a nod, with a shake of her hair and an enticing scent and with simple words she had ensnared him in her trap. Now he stood before her, hard as stone and wanting her more than he had ever wanted a woman. The urge, the need, to touch and taste and hold and have and fill and claim and mark her as his own grew until he feared it might overwhelm him. Looking around the chamber, he spied a small table with a jug and some goblets. He used it to break her spell.

"Wine, my lady?" He poured some for himself, managing not to spill it in spite of the way his hand shook. Without waiting for her reply, he filled a goblet for her and brought it to her.

"My thanks, Lord Orrick," she whispered as she lifted the wine to her mouth.

He watched as she finished her sip and as a drop of the sweet dark liquid began to trickle down from the corner of her lips. Even as his body moved forward to her, Marguerite used the tip of her tongue to catch it. He could not allow this to continue. Pulling his control around him, Orrick stepped back.

"And the reason for this meeting?"

"Why, to meet you, my lord! I know 'tis not so unusual for those of our status to marry without ever setting eyes on each other." She paused and let her gaze move over him in a provocative way. Just as he could almost feel her touch, she continued. "But His Grace, the king, allowed this breach of etiquette because we have long been friends."

"So I have heard, my lady."

There! He needed to let her know that he was no man's fool, not even the king's. He might be forced to take Henry's cast-off lover as wife, but Orrick would not pretend he did not know the real relationship between Henry and Marguerite. Not even to her, not even to assuage his own pride.

Her reaction surprised him. She stood and handed him

the cup. Walking to the door, she faced him. The soft expression on her face changed to a much harder one, one that sapped most of the beauty from her features. She stood taller and stared at him with a look that sent icy chills down his spine.

He had seen the sensual, enticing, womanly Marguerite at first.

This was the angry, controlling, warriorlike Marguerite.

"Although I owe you nothing, Orrick of Silloth, I know that you are forced to this marriage as I am and want you to know the truth."

He lifted the cup to his mouth and swallowed the wine in one mouthful. "And which truth would that be, my lady?" Did she plan to admit that she had shared the king's bed and mayhap even had his love?

"This marriage will not happen. I am somewhat sorry that you have been drawn into this misunderstanding between the king and me, so I wish to warn you of what is to come."

Was there some other plotting going on? Did the king have some punishment in mind for some imagined wrongdoing on his or his father's part? Why this sham of marriage if Henry planned to arrest him on some charge? His gut tightened and he worried about what would happen to his people if he were imprisoned or hanged. Finally, he took a breath and asked.

"And what is to come?"

"My lord Henry is simply using this charade to put me in my place. I overstepped myself and he wishes me to know what he could do if he is displeased with me. I fear you have been caught up in a lovers' quarrel."

The roiling in his stomach lessened a bit as his own suspicions grew. Would Henry go through all of this very public display of giving her in marriage and then default at the last moment? Orrick had signed most of the papers involving the transfer of property and titles and, indeed, had received a portion of the gold promised already. Aye, a king could undo all of that with a word, but would he?

"Henry will call off the wedding today?" he asked, searching for something more. His instincts told him there was much more going on here.

"Of course he will! He loves me and will not give me away to some northern lord who never attends court." She must have seen his look of disbelief for she added, "I was raised as consort for a king, not some…some…"

"Barbarian of mixed blood, my lady?"

Oh, her words had been duly reported to him just after she'd uttered them. He had chosen to ignore them for in the strange situation it was sometimes difficult to discern who said what to whom about whom. The challenge had been offered and accepted—there would be no more of the courtly niceties between them in this conversation. She did not soften her stance at all; indeed she seemed to be strengthened by the fact that he knew how she felt about him.

"Just so, my lord. Surely the king will find a more suitable match for you from among his English nobles. I fear I am far too accustomed to living at court and in my own country that it would make me too sad to move so far from it."

And too far from Henry. Those words remained unspoken, but they echoed in his head as though she had shouted them.

"Is your purpose in telling me this to force me to Henry with a request to call off this arrangement? Is that what you hope for?"

She looked away as though she was not going to answer and then turned back and met his stare. "I was simply trying to save you the humiliation of facing the court at a wedding without a bride at your side. I thought you should know that Henry will claim me and not allow you to marry me as you've been asked to do."

Her voice was soft and he could almost believe that she was sincere. For a brief moment he did believe her, and then a stab of pity tore at his heart as he realized the truth of the matter.

She believed it.

Marguerite believed that Henry would step in and stop the wedding. She was either ignorant of the arrangements already in place, or she was simply denying it to herself. He guessed that, after years of being the king's favorite, 'twas too difficult to admit that she no longer held his affections or that unofficial place of honor within the court. The gossips had not named a new paramour to the king, but it would simply be a matter of time before one was identified and took her place.

How could it feel to have lived less than a score of years and already be considered a castoff? Loved, abandoned and now given away to a stranger. From the look in her eyes and the tilt of her chin, she did not want pity from him or anyone else. So, he would give her none. But as she had warned him, he would offer one of his own.

"I, too, believe that humiliation will be the order of the day, Marguerite, but fear you will feel its bite and not I. I suggest you prepare yourself and protect your heart if you wish to survive it."

She blinked rapidly as though trying to understand, and he knew it was time to leave. He put his hand to the knob of the door and she stepped aside, allowing him to pass without comment.

There was nothing else to say to her. They were both pawns, playing out the moves of the game in front of the Plantagenet court and before the game master himself.

God help them all.

Meet Terri Brisbin

RWA RITA®-nominated, award-winning and *USA Today* best-selling author **Terri Brisbin** is a mom, a wife, grandmom(!) and a dental hygienist who has sold more than 3.5 million copies of her historical and paranormal romance novels and novellas in more than 25 countries and 20 languages. Her current and upcoming historical and paranormal/fantasy romances are published by Harlequin Historicals, Oliver Heber Books and independently, too.

Visit her website for more info about Terri, her works and upcoming events.

Connect with her on
Facebook @TerriBrisbinAuthor
X (Twitter) @Terri_Brisbin
Instagram @TerriBrisbin

TerriBrisbin.com

www.ingramcontent.com/pod-product-compliance
Lightning Source LLC
Chambersburg PA
CBHW071944190726
48293CB00004B/1330